INTO THE UNCANNY
Twelve Tales of Terror

Text copyright © 2012 - 2019 by Dorian J. Sinnott

All rights reserved. No part of this publication may be reproduced, distributed, published, or transmitted in any form or by any means without the prior written permission of the publisher and author.

Aside from actual historical persons and events, the characters and situations that surround them portrayed in this book are fictitious. Any similarity to real persons, living or dead, is coincidental and not intended by the author.

All works included in this anthology are reprints from their original publications, who own first time publication rights. Permission was granted prior to the release of this anthology.

A SINNOTT ART STUDIO PUBLICATION

Cover illustration and cover layout by WarrenDesign
Interior illustrations by Belinda Sinnott, Mark Sinnott, and Joe Sinnott

Library of Congress Cataloging-in Publication Data

Sinnott, Dorian J.

Sinnott Art Studio

ISBN: 978-1-074-85771-4

Printed in the United States of America

10 9 8 7 6 5 4 3 2 1

"Our greatest fears—the things that hide under the bed, in the closets, and in the mind— are only as real as we allow them to be."

TABLE OF CONTENTS

Murders at Whitechapel .... Page 9

Monsters .... Page 22

Death's Chess Game .... Page 25

John .... Page 33

The Beast of Bridestowe .... Page 47

Flat Line .... Page 53

Sirena .... Page 57

Isolation .... Page 62

Beyond the Pines .... Page 73

The Hunger .... Page 81

A Place of His Own .... Page 94

The Haunting of Berkeley Square .... Page 109

Murders at Whitechapel

Published in Generic Literary Zine (2012)

It was when the papers spoke of a second victim that Lawrence Caldwell decided to get on the case. It had been only about a week since the first attack by the Whitechapel Murderer, and the district papers couldn't stop talking about it. Amongst the graphic details of how Miss Chapman was brutally murdered were more assumptions of who the mysterious killer could be. Perhaps an Irish immigrant? Jew? "Pervert"? All were simply more targets to feed the imagination of gossip around Whitechapel. At least, that's how Lawrence saw it.

Adjusting the brim of his hat, Lawrence tucked the paper under his arm before heading down Wentworth Street. From the alleyways and corners, he could hear hushed whispers of the locals; women of their safety and men of the discovery of the killer so he too could be put to death. Lawrence rounded a corner into the street sellers' section of town—the area inhabited mostly by Irish immigrants. His eyes skimmed up and down the vendors, hastily catching glimpses of mothers trying to calm their children while fathers pushed sales on the English. Most waved the vendors off and continued on their way, muttering comments of how filthy the families were. Yet, Lawrence didn't stop until he reached a small stand towards the end of the street. Only then did he smile and hold out two farthings.

"I'll take the usual." Lawrence watched as the man behind the stand glanced up.

He had mussed auburn hair hidden beneath his newsboy cap and hundreds of freckles dotted his pale cheeks. He appeared to be in his early thirties, much like Lawrence himself. Wiping a few beads of sweat out from under his cap, he smiled back.

"I've been waiting for you all afternoon, Lawrence." The man tossed the fresh fruit to him before adding the farthings to his pouch. "I was beginning to worry you wouldn't show. You're one of the only Englishmen to come through here and actually purchase something."

"You're my friend, Oscar." Lawrence took a bite out of the fruit. "Though others may find it odd, you're forgetting that I have Irish blood in me, as well. My mother's side."

Oscar snorted. "At least you have the English blood to make up for it with your father."

Lawrence said nothing at that, simply smirking before changing the topic. "Have you heard the latest news of the Whitechapel Murderer?"

"That they're suspecting he's an Irishman? Yes, I believe I did hear talk of that earlier today." Oscar shifted in the seat at his stand. "Why?"

10

Lawrence unfolded the paper from under his arm, holding it out to Oscar. When the immigrant stared blankly at the front page, Lawrence annotated it to him.

"There was another victim last night. Miss Annie Chapman. They say there was a witness this time, at least someone having seen her speaking with a gentleman."

"Don't they have suspects yet? You would think the police would be on top of that." Oscar said once his eyes lifted from the artwork provided in the paper.

"They have suspicion, yes. All they've mentioned is thought of it being perhaps an immigrant of some sort, as… you had mentioned. That or a *"pervert"*." The word slipped off Lawrence's tongue in reluctance as Oscar snorted. "Honestly, I think otherwise."

"What do you suggest we do, Lawrence? We're not the law. We're ordinary men."

"As very well could the murderer be." Lawrence looked Oscar over again before smiling. "Why don't you come by my place tonight for a drink? We'll discuss my thoughts there."

After a moment of hesitation, Oscar finally nodded in agreement. Lawrence took another bite from the fruit as he bid farewell, flicking his trench coat before heading on his way through the already darkening alley.

"It has to be someone with at least some education." Lawrence poured another glass of gin for Oscar. "The wounds the victims

11

suffered from both before and after death were too intricate to be just anyone."

"A surgeon perhaps?" Oscar took a swig of the alcohol once he got situated on the posh couch in the center of the room.

While Lawrence wasn't of the highest class in the city, his home clearly showed evidence of wealth from several generations. A candlelit chandelier hung from the ceiling over a wooden floor carpeted in fine imported rugs from India. Even the walls were papered in gaudy patterns, cluttering the mind if stared at for too long.

"They certainly needed knowledge of anatomy." Lawrence took a seat beside Oscar. "The murderer didn't *just* cut his victims open for the thrill of it, either. Some of the interior organs were also removed and missing. Only someone with a history in medical procedures could have located them all..."

Oscar's hand slid over to Lawrence's knee, resting upon it gently. "Obviously they would need to be wealthy then, hm? Or at least well off." He gave a little squeeze.

"Well, that removes all questioning of the immigrants, then. For the most part anyway." Lawrence could notice Oscar's eyes lower at that for a brief moment, until he managed a smirk.

"It still leaves the "perverts" on trial, however."

Lawrence moved closer to Oscar, a gleam in his eye. Parting his lips with a soft chuckle, he, too, forced a smile. "Now what would a "pervert" want with women?"

Oscar scoffed in return, feeling Lawrence remove his glass of gin from his hands and set it on the table beside them. Leaning in, Lawrence closed his eyes and allowed his lips to catch Oscar's, the candles of the chandelier dimming for the night.

It wasn't long after the death of Miss Chapman that a new article struck the front page. The once called Whitechapel Murderer now had a new name, supposedly proclaimed by himself due to a letter that to the police: "Jack the Ripper". The people of Whitechapel were now talking more than ever before. Not only had the killer released a letter with his supposed alias, but also details of what his next victim would experience.

"I can't possibly see why he would send such a thing." Lawrence sipped his tea as he read the front page, glancing up at Oscar momentarily. "Much of it sounds forced. It hardly reads like a killer wrote it."

"Well, you did say that he very well could be an ordinary man." Oscar watched his friend with interest. "It also seems he was quite taken aback by the press commenting on the skills of a doctor. Perhaps, if it were him, he fears the authorities are getting closer?"

"That or whoever wrote it wants to keep the minorities as the main target. It's all rather confusing. If this *were* the killer, why would he send a note to the police? And if it's *not* the killer, why would anyone send such a letter claiming they were?" Lawrence stared at the paper in perplexity.

"Like you said, if it *is* the killer, we know he's planning to strike again… just the details of his next victim. But if not…" Oscar bit his lip.

"This very well could lead to another murder."

The street lamps flickered as Lawrence and Oscar made their ways home. Shadows lingered on the cold cobblestone streets, the only sounds coming from gin-shops and opium dens along the alleys. Both men's shoes clicked along the street beneath them, echoing off the dark buildings. As they continued along, Lawrence could feel Oscar's fingertips begin to curl around his own, causing him to pull away sharply.

"We can't, Oscar," was all Lawrence said before pushing his hands into the pockets of his trench coat. "You know the law."

"Oh, come now, Lawrence! No one's around! Take a look for yourself!"

Lawrence feigned a glimpse over his shoulder through the darkness as he heaved a sigh. "It's best we don't risk it. All it takes is one person to see before we—"

"Before we get marked as the "*perverts*" who have been committing the murders?" Oscar snorted.

"Before we end up on *trial* or in *prison* for such being ourselves."

Oscar fell silent. Without another word from either of them, both men continued down the street. Only when they crossed over onto Mitre Square was their silence broken, when hollers from a policeman ahead of them caught their attention. Hurrying down the square, Lawrence and Oscar stopped short, the officer, too, looking distraught.

The body of a woman lay before them—mutilated. Like the other victims in the previous cases, her throat had been slit open, blood pouring out over the cobblestones. But that wasn't what took both Lawrence and Oscar back. It was her abdomen, completely cut open, intestines stretched up over her shoulder, which caused them to grimace and turn away.

"Did either of you see what happened? Anything suspicious? Anything at all?" The officer began questioning Lawrence and Oscar once other authorities arrived to look at the body.

"Nothing at all, sir." Lawrence spoke softly with a tremble in his breath. "We didn't even hear a scream."

As the officers surrounded the body and allowed their doctor to observe the aftermath, Lawrence and Oscar turned away again. Had only they been passing through less than a half hour earlier, they would have run into the murderer themselves.

"Catherine Eddowes wasn't the only one murdered, Oscar. It appears an Elizabeth Stride was also attacked last night, presumably by the same killer." Lawrence's hands were shaky as he held the paper now, leaning against a wall for support.

"What?" Even Oscar's voice carried a trace of disgruntlement. "He's never struck twice in one night."

"I wouldn't be surprised if this was due to the letter. Like you said, if it wasn't a sign from the killer himself, it was sure to spark something." Lawrence folded the paper before tossing it in the nearby trashcan. "What I find especially peculiar is that Miss Eddowes's ear was sliced and a chunk was taken off the lobe."

"A lot was taken off of her, Lawrence. Surely you can remember." Oscar trembled at the thought.

"Yes... but if you remember correctly, in the letter that was written to the police, this, "Jack the Ripper", made sure to note that his next victim would have a piece of their ear removed."

Oscar peered over to Lawrence steadily as more hushed whispers rose around them from passersby who had just received their copy of the paper. Glancing out across the street filled with its bustling horse-drawn carriages, Lawrence parted his lips.

"Either it truly was the killer who sent the note as a forewarning... or someone playing what they thought would be a joke may have just gotten an innocent woman killed."

Though the weeks passed, neither Lawrence nor Oscar could wipe the thoughts of Miss Eddowes's body from their minds.

They still saw the blood, covering the once gray cobblestone; still saw her intestines, coiled around her arm like bloody snakes squeezing the life from their prey; and they still saw her limbs, twisted and mangled against the ground. At night, they would lay awake in each other's arms, staring at the shadows on the wall. Every now and again, they could swear they shaped into the image of the ripper, looming over their bedside with his dagger ready to claim their throats as well. It was at that point, they swore they were going mad.

"Gin's not going to help drown out the thoughts, Lawrence." Oscar spoke softly as he was handed a glass from the bartender. "If anything, it's going to just add to the lack of sanity we've had these past nights."

"Please, Oscar," Lawrence coaxed, taking his glass and downing what he could of the alcohol, "it will help ease our thoughts, even if for a brief while. Enough to let us sleep tonight."

The voices of other drunken men rose up from inside the gin-shop as Oscar leaned close to Lawrence's ear, whispering. "All it will take is us stumbling around drunk blabbering what we saw the other night to get us locked up, Lawrence. We'd make the perfect image for what they're looking for in the ripper."

Oscar motioned to their reflection across the bar. He sat in his typical immigrant attire, Irish features prominent in the lighting. As for Lawrence, with his trench coat and hat, he looked much like the drawings of what the murderer was described as—especially if he were to be silhouetted by shadows.

"We need to be careful, Lawrence."

Staring at his drink, Lawrence shrugged Oscar off, taking his next glass and gulping it down to drown out his memories.

Down the dark cobbled streets, Oscar led Lawrence. While the streetlamps flared as they did every night, the men became aware of the uncanny that came with their glow. It had practically been a month since they had wandered out after dark, and the memories of the murder of Catherine Eddowes still remained prominent in their minds.

Unlike most of the nights the two spent together in public, Oscar held onto Lawrence, supporting him along the cobblestones his foot slipped upon every once in a while. His breath reeked of alcohol, the source of his staggered movements. As they rounded a corner, Oscar sighed, tugging at Lawrence's coat a bit harder now.

"You'd better hope no one spots us out here, Lawrence." He urged his friend on down the street, knowing that the sooner they arrived home, the better it was for the both of them. "With the ripper cases, policemen are everywhere. All we'd need is a slip from you, and—"

"Oh, *do* be quiet, Oscar." Even Lawrence's speech was somewhat slurred. "We'll be fine. If either of us should be worrying about being caught by the police for anything, it would be you before me."

Oscar stopped. "Why's that?"

"You worry they're out looking for good ol' Jack and that they'll turn us in for suspects. It's the immigrants they've been after, Oscar! They'd take one look at you and—"

"Well what about *you*?" Oscar glared at Lawrence. "You've got the outfit people have grown to fear thanks to the brilliant artists who have been trying to terrorize the city! Plus, you're drunk, Lawrence! They'd say you've gone mad from intoxication!"

"Think logically here, Oscar." Lawrence's voice had dropped and his eyes bitterly stared at the Irishman. "If they had to turn in either you or me for imprisonment and execution, it would be filth like you that would go first… not a higher class Englishman like me."

Oscar pressed his lips together tightly, not bothering to come back with a response. He knew that Lawrence was right, even if he was speaking through a drunken mind with no knowledge of how hurtful his words had been. They both remained in complete silence, just staring at each other, until a scream from down the street caught their attention. It was a woman.

Yet, Lawrence and Oscar simply stood there and listened, the scream burrowing deep into the backs of their minds as it longed to be forgotten along with the body of Miss Eddowes. And thus, they turned and walked away.

Monsters

Published in The Bleeding Lion Literary Magazine (2015)

I awake to the screaming—
Melody of monsters and ghouls hidden in the shadows,
Within the closet, beneath the bed.
A sea of darkness spiraling from the corners,
Beckoning for your soul.

I wish you weren't so afraid.

I pull you close, blanketing your fear.
"Monsters aren't real," I say. "They only live in our minds."
Your eyes feign belief—
A lifetime of living horrors proving me wrong.
But still,
I take your hand and take you back—

Take you back to your bedroom,
Flood the floor in the soft light of your lamp,
Checking the shadows, the closet, the bed.
"No monsters here," I say. "Not while I'm here."

The lights go out and I am left alone.

It hurts me to lie to you,
To tell you the monsters aren't real.
That they don't exist.
But I don't want you to become like I am—
Shattered, broken, devoid of all hope.

Melancholy is my only friend,
The glimmer of light that gets me through the night.
Keeping the monsters at bay.

That's why I have to fight to keep the light inside you alive,
Keep that sparkle in your eyes,
Reminding me there's a flame burning within.
A beacon.

Don't be like me.
Don't lose your light.
The truth is, when you do, the monsters *do* become real.
They just travel to the darkness.
They live inside yourself.

Death's Chess Game

Published in The Hungry Chimera Magazine (2018)

The day young Thomas Whitmore died, there was no mourning. Instead, everything in the boy's room was turned to white. The curtains were drawn open to let in the newfound light, and nurse maids changed the linen on his bed. Even the lilies left by his mother upon his nightstand bloomed anew—brighter than ever. Yet, while his mother and father wept, they were tears of joy. For the day young Thomas Whitmore died, he was reborn.

In the moments prior, only darkness had settled behind his eyes when he drew his final breath. Hallways of endless shadows paved with blind memories. No longer could he hear the whispers of his loved ones—for they'd been drowned out by silence. The only voice amidst the endless void was the beckon of Death. And Thomas refused to heed.

A boy on the cusp of thirteen, he knew well enough that there was still life to live. Death had come too soon, and with each of his calls, Thomas turned away.

"My time has not come," he repeatedly stated. "Come again for me when I've grown old."

"Your time has run out," Death replied, "and I do not cater only to the elderly."

Thomas faced Death once more with a burning resentment deep in his eyes. Perhaps, to Death, the only kindle of life that still remained. That the boy still clung to.

"But you cannot have me," Thomas said. "I have much to live for. Much to see. My life has barely begun."

Death shook his head. "I'm afraid Life lost that match, my friend. I am the master when it comes to a good game of chess. Why, the pieces usually fall right into my lap."

"So why not let me play? Why must Life wager my soul when I, myself, should be the one betting it?" Thomas asked. "Surely I am a far better master than you."

There was a hesitant pause before Death drew a smile. "Well, you certainly have a strong spirit, dear boy. But, I'm afraid you, nor anyone else for that matter, is a match for me. When I am called, I always win."

Thomas straightened himself up and locked his gaze with Death. "And I only play to win. And I, too, have never lost."

"You just won't budge, will you?" Death asked, Thomas remaining still. "Very well. But one game. One chance. That's all you get."

"That's all I need."

Death's pieces were built of bone, the board icy to the touch, as Thomas was certain his body had become. With a swift motion of his hand, Death instructed Thomas to command the pieces of white.

"A slight advantage," Death jeered. "After all, it's Life that gets the first move in the game. Death just follows."

Thomas took a seat across from Death, eying his pieces intently. The opening play was the most important. It was the building block to all that came after—the fate of the game. Carefully guiding his hand, he chose his first move.

"Pawn to d4."

"Setting up for a Queen's Gambit?" Death had seen this move many times in his matches against Life—the sacrifice of one to keep another thriving.

"Hardly."

And wrong indeed Death was. An impenetrable wall of defense soon lined Thomas's side of the board—playing gambits of its own only to lash back and take Death's strongest pieces. But Death didn't hesitate. He simply smiled and continued making his moves—slowly bringing down the barrier and closing in on his target: the white king—the beacon of Life.

"Even the strongest forces can't keep me out," Death said. "Your wall was well played, but time erodes the foundation and makes it weak."

"Weakness doesn't mean defeat," Thomas replied; and sure enough, he countered the damage he had taken. "Defeat is only when you give in."

Death shook his head with a slight grin. "My, your fortitude truly is one to admire."

The game dragged on for what felt like hours, the chill of the air rising off the pieces and numbing Thomas's fingers. He could sense a stalemate with each of Death's moves, but he wasn't about to have it. *In a game for Life*, he thought, *there can be no ties with Death*. With the careful slide of his hand to move a lone pawn, Thomas nudged the rook beside it, just enough so it touched the adjacent square. One move closer to locking in Death's king.

He continued with this trick a few more times, carefully watching to see if Death had taken notice. Yet, not a word was spoken. Thomas was certain he had overseen it. Gliding his rook across the polished bone board, Thomas allowed a smile to tug at his lips.

"Check."

There was no expression of shock from Death. Not even a question of how it could have been possible. *Life never gets this far*, Thomas thought. *Shouldn't Death be surprised at least? Somewhat taken aback?*

The only response that the boy was met with, however, was a correction. "That's Check*mate*, boy."

Thomas leaned forward to inspect the board, confirming what Death had stated was true.

"Ah!" he exclaimed. "So it is! Well then…"

His eyes scanned Death, waiting for a reply. A congratulations. Anything. Instead, he was met only with the very silence he had awoken to when Life had bid him farewell—leaving him to the darkness.

"An honorary game, I'll give you that. Perhaps I was wrong about you… You fight for Life far stronger than many I've seen," Death said after a moment. "Therefore, as we agreed, I leave you to bask in her light until we are to meet again. When you have, as you offered, 'grown old'. "

Thomas nodded with a smile, but gave no reply.

As he stood and began to walk away from the board, towards the faint beacon of light at the end of the darkness, Death called out to him. This time, however, his voice wasn't as embracing as it was when he first beckoned him. The deep, dry tone was chilling, and it caused Thomas to stop.

"I should warn you, though, dear boy… There is a price to be paid."

"A price?" Thomas asked. "What do you mean?"

"When one cheats against Death, one also cheats against Life. Don't think I didn't sense your moves back there—a simple flick of the wrist, the nudge of a knuckle. Crafty, I give you that. Determined." The churning in Thomas's gut was unbearable.

"But, as I said, Life and Death are intertwined. More alike than you may think. I think our very game has proven that to you."

"So what will you do? What price must I pay?" Thomas tried to shake the quiver from his voice. "Surely there is no greater punishment than Death."

"But there is, my boy." Death motioned to light at the far end of the void. "Life."

With a strained gasp, Thomas awoke to the endless white of his bedroom. The sounds of late spring were upon him, drifting in through the opened window. His parents and nurse maid embraced him, their tears of joy welcoming him back to the wonders of Life. Born anew, with no signs of ailing. Of pain. Young Thomas appeared to have never fallen within Death's grasp.

A dream, Thomas convinced himself, *that's all it had been. A deep slumber I fell into; a state of comatose, playing with my inner demons. A match against myself. My nightmares. My fears. Death, no, he never came for me.*

Yet, as the years passed and Thomas grew, he began to deny his initial thought. While he was blessed with good health and radiant Life, those around him fell to Death. First his mother, only a year after his reawakening—taken in the night suddenly, without warning. Then his tutors and dear friends. His father had been next, on the eve of Thomas's twentieth birthday. One by one, they disappeared. Claimed by Death, but not strategic enough to win their way back to Life's side of the board.

It was only when Thomas finally married a young woman, Emily, a few towns over, he thought the curse to be gone. They lived alone in happiness, never witnessing Death's cruel touch. They had a daughter, a new seed of Life, and the rays of warmth that Thomas felt were never stronger. It was, as he claimed, as if he were once more reborn through her—perhaps more-so than through Death. *Happiness*, he thought, *that's what Life is. That's what really living feels like.*

But on that cold and rainy night, Death did come to claim another. The young baby girl's cries had ceased and silence overtook the house. There was no light. No warmth. And the tears shed weren't as his parents' had been all those years ago. He and Emily stood over the vacant crib and wept. Prayed. But Death never returned the child.

"It isn't right. It isn't fair!" Thomas cried. "Why punish those I love? Why take Life from their veins? It was I that cheated you, Death. *I* that stood against you. So why? Why take them instead of me?"

Thomas explained to Emily the story of a young boy on the brink of Death, playing a game of chess to win back his chance for Life. A story that he had believed for years to only be a dream. But as he took her warm hands in his icy cold ones, he could see the look of fear in her eyes.

"You see," Thomas said, "In order to get to the king, one must go through the pawns. And, one by one, they'll disappear. Then when the king is left alone, with no way to win on his own, the game is over. Life, is indeed, the cruelest punishment. For you must stand by and watch as each of the other pieces are taken; and you are left defenseless. Running. One square at a time. *Praying* that Death can't catch up to you."

His voice grew shaky as he released Emily's hand. Again, he allowed the tears to come; this time, however, for himself.

"It's just like a game of chess, Life and Death. They're both the same pieces, just painted different colors on opposite ends of the board. Cheat at one, you pay for the consequence in the other. You may think when you, the small pawn, reaches the end of the board, you are given a chance of glory. To be reborn a queen. But in the end, you realize the truth."

Thomas looked into Emily's eyes.

"She always returns to Life with Death's shadow to her back."

John

Published in Coffin Bell Journal (2018)

Brown eyes stare back at me through the glass. They live in my reflection, but I know they're not my own. For as long as I've remembered, they were a light blue grey; but over the last month of living with the Yates' family, I've watched them change.

Now, don't get me wrong. I've heard stories of eye colors that fall into the hazel spectrum, changing color in the differing light or colors surrounding. "Chameleon eyes" I always called them—only they seemed to stand out more when contrasting colors complimented them rather than feign disguise. But for me, this was not the case. I did not have hazel eyes and I never suspected I would. Yet, here I stood before the bathroom mirror, picking apart the deep, chocolate brown that took over my once light eyes.

And that's when the panic set in.

There had been other slight changes I'd noticed over the course of the last few weeks, all signs I had taken as growing older. More mature. For one, the freckles that lined my cheeks vanished beneath the milky surface of my skin, never rearing themselves again. Not even in the strongest sunlight. As for another, I'd shrunken about two inches. I brushed it off as an error on the pediatrician's part. The doctors called to Marble Oaks Children's Home weren't the most thorough after all, and I had heard numerous adoptees having changes in height after being settled into their new homes. But now, I wasn't so sure.

There always were rumors about Marble Oaks being a shady place—an orphan asylum that practiced techniques from the "dark ages" as they'd say. I'd never seen anything questionable during my three years there. If asked, the only thing that could come to mind was the floors were too creaky and in winter, it was too cold and damp. But the caregivers did all they could to keep us comfortable and help us get placed in our forever homes. Most of the time, we all did. It was rare having any child "age out" there. They simply seemed to know which families would be the right fit.

But maybe I fit too well, I think to myself as I continue staring at my reflection. Maybe I was the perfect solution to the Yates' childless home. I'd been receiving comments from family friends I'd meet, saying how "hard it was to tell I was even adopted", that I "could pass as a biological Yates so well." I always thought it was flattery. Everyone knows the first few weeks after adoption are awkward—especially when you're thirteen like me.

The more I come to think of it though, the more I realize how right people were.

Some of my features seemed more like Christine and Jonathon Yates' as each week went by. I'd heard it was common: adoptees tend to mold into their new families over time. *But never like this,* I think. Since when would my parents'—biological—light eyes turn into the Yates' dark brown? That was unheard of.

I uncap my pill bottle and remove my focus from the image in the glass. There are only a few chalky white pills left since my dose had been upped. *I'll need it refilled soon*, I remind myself, shaking two capsules out into the palm of my hand.

    I'd always suffered from chronic headaches over the years—shooting pain through the temple and down into my eye. It was almost unbearable at times. I'd taken the medication for a while now, but once my scheduled adoption came closer, the migraines became worse. So, upon being sent home, I was ordered a heavier dose.

    "Two pills in the morning, two at night."

    It was a prescription the doctor said, in case the pain returned full force again. He knew well I didn't want that, and my new family certainly didn't either. Illness is failure in the life of a child like me—in the system. The healthy get homes and keep them. The sick age out and are returned. The last thing I wanted was to be dropped back off at Marble Oaks like a defective toy.

    "May I get a refund? Or maybe make an exchange?"

    I know the Yates' would never actually do that, but fear sometimes got the best of me.

With a gulp of water from the sink, I wash the pills down. I dry my mouth on the back of my hand, glancing to the doorway when I hear a rapping against it.

"John, dear, aren't you coming down for dinner?"

My adoptive mother looks in at me cautiously and I nod my head after a moment's hesitation. It's so weird hearing her call me that… "John", not "dear". Prior to my adoption, my name had been "Thomas"—one I actually preferred. But with the legal changing of my last name to their family name, they pleaded I take the name they chose to give me. A "tribute" to my adoptive father. Jonathon.

"He always wanted a child named after him," my adoptive mother chirped.

I didn't want to cause controversy, especially so soon after everything became official. So, I did as they wanted and changed my name.

The only real struggle was getting used to being called "John" instead of "Thomas".

"Be sure to be down soon. You don't want your plate getting cold." I could tell she was trying too hard in her kindness. "Your father already ate… he said he wasn't feeling too well, but everything is still set up for you."

Again I give her a nod. Sometimes I'm at a loss for words, and my adoptive family was the hardest to speak to. It was just awkward, and I wanted everything to be right. Perfect. *No returns…*

The light must have hit me just right in that moment. From her throat I could hear a little gasp of enthusiasm, followed by a comment I wasn't expecting.

"Your eyes look lovely this evening," she says. "There's just something about them… oh, I must sound ridiculous…"

I take a moment before I respond. "Thank you…"

Even in the dim bathroom light, she knows they're brown. I feel it.

After dinner, I find myself pacing the halls. My mother has turned in and I know Father wasn't feeling well. Being up and walking around takes my mind off the worry of my eyes—at least for the moment. Questions still fill my head as to why such a thing could have happened. Perhaps a side effect of my medication? Stress? Or maybe it really was just puberty setting in.

I continue with my mindless wandering until I spot a door I don't recall seeing before. I know I'd only been living here for a little over a month, but some of the home's layout I still wasn't fully familiar with. It wouldn't have caught my interest at all had it not been for the green and blue woodblock lettering hammered into the door.

"JOHN'S ROOM"

My room is on the other end of the hall, right next to the bathroom. It was made clear to me on move in that that was where I would stay.

"The perfect room for our little Johnny."

I approach the door, reaching out to give the knob a twist—just to peek inside—when my adoptive father's voice catches me off guard.

"John. What are you doing?"

I freeze in place, unsure what to say. While coming out and asking what was hidden behind the door clearly could have been an easy answer, part of me worried it was a private room. My father's. After all, his name is Jonathon, too—only by birth. I remain still and quiet and he motions me over.

"Why don't you get some rest, son? You look awfully tired."

The physical exhaustion has yet to hit, but I can't deny my emotional and mental drainage. There was only so much staring into a mirror at myself I could do in one right. And so, I nod to my father and return to my assigned room.

"John's Room" never crossed my mind again for the next few weeks. I was too busy getting acquainted with other family members that came and went, and working to get into a school. The local schools were on break for the winter holidays, and filing for my new attendance was postponed—to my family's displeasure anyway. The only thing I took note of during that time was my physical appearances, again slowly changing.

My eyes never went back to their original blue shade. They remained dark brown, my hair soon following. All my life the locks had been a honey chestnut shade, but as the weeks went on, the tints of red only became darker. Even my nose was turning up and my jaw line becoming more prominent. *Puberty?* The more I saw the changes, the less I could believe that's what it truly was.

It's getting to the point I don't recognize myself in the mirror anymore.

I struggle carrying the last box of my belongings up the shaky attic stairs. One of my old sweaters almost slips from inside and I grunt as I tug it back in. The Yates' had replaced my hand-me-down wardrobe and suggested I store it for further donation to those less fortunate—most likely back to Marble Oaks. I, however, could have argued otherwise. Some of the clothes were in bad enough shape the first time around. I pitied whichever child ended up with them.

The attic is dark and damp and I can feel the cold rake through me as I search for a place to set the box. Other piles of boxes line the corners, so I give in and decide to place it amongst them. I'm careful with my steps along the boards, shifting the box into place between a mess of others. With the force and angle, however, one of the others beside it tips over and I groan when the contents strew themselves across the floor.

I quickly begin gathering the items—baby toys—and tossing them back into the box. *A collection of old memories*, I assume, *kept to remember the childhood.* I continue placing the toys inside until I spot a photograph that had fallen out. My eyes skim over to it, steadily, and that's when I feel the chill of the attic take hold.

It's a portrait, of a boy no older than thirteen. His dark brown hair and eyes stare back at me through the photo and his smile is haunting. I run a shaky finger down the image of his face and swallow the knot forming in my throat.

The boy is me.

But, I don't remember ever having taken that picture. Sure, Marble Oaks photographed us from time-to-time, keeping our records updated for potential families interested in us; but they were never this professional. And I never owned the clothing in the photo.

And that's when it sunk in. My hair and eyes were never brown until I started living at the Yates' house.

I tremble and quickly shove the photo back into the box of toys. I feel the acid sliding up my throat and my stomach twists and lurches. From over the box flap, I can see the backside of the photo now, a remark etched into it.

"John, March '93"

Eight months before I met the Yates'. I've only been living here since November.

I stand before the door I seemed to have forgotten about weeks ago, continuing to feel the knot inside me tighten. I know I can't hold back any more, and I need to face my fears—all of which are my adoptive family discovering my snooping. But I don't let it worry me. I turn the knob and push into the room, unsure of what I'll find. *More baby toys?*

A mechanical beeping is what my ears are met with—a signal soon to flatline.

The room is decorated much like any child's my age, the walls painted dark blue, allowing for little light to enter. Toys and school awards line the shelves along with happy family photos, framed for memory. But the machinery makes me sick— hospital equipment strung up to the bed. To a boy my age.

I slowly approach him, my heart beating rapidly against my chest. The closer I get, the better I can see his face. *My* face. At least what my face has become. It's like looking down at your corpse after the soul leaves the body. A frightening, disgusting feeling. And I can't shake it.

The boy's eyes remain shut as I stand there, no trace of acknowledgement to my presence. He's in a deep coma, that much I'm sure of, but why I don't understand. There's *so much* I don't understand. I take a step back, unable to look any more, when I hear my adoptive mother's fake, honeyed voice trail through the hall.

"John, dear, you haven't taken your medication this morning. You know the doctor's orders."

My medication.

I clench my fists at the thought. Those white pills I'd been tormented by for the last three months. They never did help my migraines. In fact, I swore they made them worse. The only thing I'd ever noticed them make amends to was my face. My body. My eyes, my hair, my skin. It was never migraine medication I'd been taking. And it was clear to me now.

"John, dear."

When I look to the doorway, my mother is standing there, almost as pale as I am. She calls out for me again, motioning me over to her, but I remain still. I can feel my body shaking from anger and fear.

"John…"

"My name's *Thomas*," I snap at her, correcting her for the first time. I don't care if it's no longer legal—that's the name my parents gave me. And that was the name I was going to take with me to my grave.

"Oh, John, darling, don't be angry. It breaks my heart to see you so upset…" My adoptive mother's voice was getting more and more forced by the second.

"Why didn't you tell me?" I manage to choke out.

"Tell you what, dear?"

I point a shaky finger to the bed. To the boy hooked up to every machine imaginable. To *John*.

"We didn't want to hurt you, baby. Why grow attached to a brother so little for this world? You don't deserve that pain," she says.

"*Brother?*" My fists clench again. "He's not my *brother!*"

"Now, now... don't say that..."

"No!" My voice is growing louder by the second. "He's not. He's the mold you used to turn me into your 'perfect little child'. Just to replace the one you lost."

"Oh, John..." My mother's voice drops slightly. "Marble Oaks is fit for parents grieving over the loss of a child—or, a soon-to-be loss of a child. Adoption can help amend the heart's wounds when—"

"This *isn't* adoption!" I'm yelling now. "What you're doing is *sick*."

"We did nothing, dear. We simply went with what options were given to us, and Marble Oaks seemed like the best. They promised they could fit us with a child, one that would match perfectly to the family. Sure, they said you were all a bit ill and needed proper medication before you could come home... but it was worth it in the end. They needed to prepare you for the big change."

I don't know how much more of this I can take.

"You see, all we had to do was bring in a photograph of our dear John. They assured us they would find someone to fill his shoes, and they found you. You were practically the same height and build, and just the right age. Countless blood samples and graphing from our boy it took, but when they sent you home with your upped doses... My! You really were fitting right in. A *true* member of the Yates family."

I shake my head.

"And before long, you'll be completely adjusted. Perfect. No one will ever know."

I open my mouth to say something, but my father is in the doorway, syringe in hand. I tense up, beginning to back away but he's faster than I am, and he grabs onto my arm and holds me tight. I squirm but it's not enough.

"It's alright, dear. You just need some rest to sleep everything off. I'm sure you'll be fine in the morning."

The needle slips beneath my skin and I let out a cry of pain as the burning sensation pulses through my blood. The boy with the monitors hooked up to him is the last thing I see before I give in and sleep.

It's been a year since my mother and father said I hit my head in the accident. They told me I was in a coma for a while, unaware of the world around me—trapped within my own. Most memories before my awakening are gone, living on only through photographs. But I tell myself I remember. Maybe it's because I've really convinced myself that I do, or because I want to impress my parents and give them hope. Or, maybe I really am starting to recall memories of before. Amnesia is funny like that.

I hear my mother call for me downstairs and I respond back with a, "just a minute!"

I uncap the bottle of my daily vitamin pills, washing them down quickly, as not to hold Mother up any longer. We're going shopping today with my aunt and she doesn't want to be late. I hate taking them, but the doctor said the vitamins are rich and natural and may help me with my memories. I'm not sure how much I believe of it, but I keep taking them to make my parents happy. *Give them hope.*

"John, dear!"

"I'm coming!"

I close the medicine cabinet and take a glimpse at my reflection in the mirror. My dark brown eyes stare back at me, full of life. They're beautiful. Perfect. My father's eyes. Yet, even in their bright glow, I always find myself questioning.

Why does it feel like I'm looking at a stranger in the mirror?

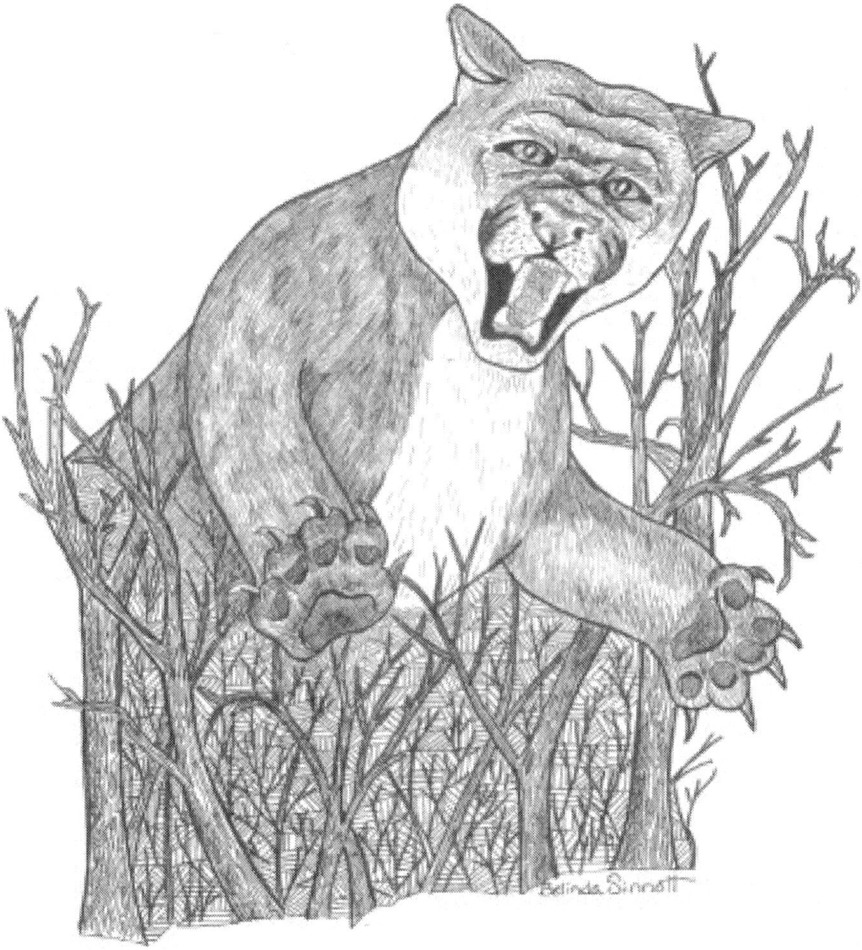
Belinda Sinnott

The Beast of Bridestowe

Published in Spill Yr Guts Horror Zine (2018)

It was when the snow had fallen fresh upon Bridestowe that Finch noted their return. Large, cat-like paw prints trailed away from the farm house, leading towards the forest just beyond the village border. Specks of crimson blood stained the snow, carnal remains of livestock littering the field. Finch heaved a breath and drew the door shut.

"It's back," was all that was uttered from his lips that morning at breakfast.

His wife Elizabeth sat in silenced shock. Dabbing her lips with her handkerchief, she finally cleared her throat. Finch ran his fingers through his hair.

"I checked the barn… There isn't a sheep left."

"Not any?" Elizabeth pursed her lips when her husband shook his head. "We'll make do until the spring thaw. I can always go into town. The butcher is sure to have lamb. And don't forget, we have the hens."

"That isn't the point, Lizzie."

Finch stared bitterly into the small flame of the candle in the center of the table. The flickers reflected in his deep green eyes. Elizabeth was taken aback when he spoke again.

"I'm going after it."

"Going after it?"

"The beast."

"Beast? Oh, please, dear… Not with the stories again. Everyone knows the beast is simply a myth."

"It's no myth, Lizzie. I've seen it myself, with my own two eyes."

"Dear…"

Finch shook his head. "There's nothing left. And it's not going to stop. When it comes back looking for more, what do you think it will hunt?"

Elizabeth was silent. Feeling her husband's hand gently brush against hers, she glanced at him.

"I can't risk it hurting you," he said. "Or… Edward."

Upon hearing a creak, Finch turned his attention to the stairwell. Through the mid-morning shadows, he could make out the small stature of a young boy. He stood still, simply listening and watching the conversation at the dinner table. Finch stared at him for a moment longer, then looked back to Elizabeth.

"I'll bring its body back. We'll mount it if we must! But I will. I'll make it pay."

Elizabeth shook her head. "Please…"

"Don't worry. I'll be alright. I promise."

He could see the worry on her face, but he gave her hand an assuring squeeze.

"I'll be back by nightfall."

Twigs snapped under Finch's feet as he ventured through the thick groves of Whistman's Woods. The trees snaked around him in thick mangles, making it difficult to see in the distance. A light fog hovered amongst the branches, cloaking the moss blanketed boulders that lined the paths. The snow had barely fallen beneath the shelter of the trees. Only a light dusting rest upon the fallen leaves. Finch took another step forward, listening for any signs of movement around him. The forest was still.

"Papa." The young boy's voice was the first to break the silence as Finch tugged him along. "Where are we going?"

Finch didn't stop, even when his son staggered over the roots jutting from the forest floor. He kept his lips tight for a few moments before finally responding gruffly.

"To find the beast."

"Mama says the beast is just a story…"

"It's no story, Edward. Anyone in Bridestowe could tell you that. And anyone would agree with me that it needs to be destroyed."

"But… why?"

"It killed our sheep. Now we've nothing left to get us through the winter."

The young boy looked up at his father slowly. "Maybe it was hungry."

"Edward…" Finch closed his eyes. "Hungry or not, it's driving us to starvation. And if it returns, a fate far worse."

Edward lowered his head in thought. He shuffled his feet, feeling the grip on his wrist tighten. Finch gave him a sharp tug and led him towards a thicket of trees. The silence still stirred around them, becoming more deafening the further they headed. Snaking shadows crept along the earth, causing Edward to flinch. Once more he glanced up to his father.

"How are you going to catch it?"

Finch continued looking straight ahead, now gripping the rifle over his shoulder as he walked, his other hand still tightly gripping his son.

"We'll need to bait it," he replied. "The beast is a hunter. He won't show himself for just anything."

"Why didn't we bring a sheep?" Edward asked.

The bitterness in Finch's eyes returned yet again. "There are no more sheep…"

Edward flinched as his father's nails dug into his skin slightly. "T-then how will we bait it?"

Through the trees, Finch could make out a clearing. Straightening his posture with confidence, he responded.

"We'll think of something…"

The sun began to sink in the sky, darkness setting upon the forest. Finch sat with his rifle loaded, resting on his lap, while Edward paced nervously. He looked to his father only once, biting his lower lip in thought.

"Papa… Didn't Mama want us back before sunset?"

His father didn't look at him.

"She wanted *me* back before nightfall, as I promised. I hardly think she knows you came along."

"I... just wanted to help..."

Finch glanced up from his rifle and over to where Edward stood. The young boy trembled both from the fear and the cold the evening was bringing upon him. A smile tugged at Finch's lips as he nodded.

"You will, Edward."

Through the thicket, the snapping of twigs rose up. Finch averted his gaze from his son, spotting a pair of golden eyes glinting through the darkness. His shoulders tensed as he hushed his son, motioning through the branches.

"Be still."

Edward froze at his father's words. His eyes remained fixed on the rifle Finch kept in his lap, watching as it was slowly raised. A low growl sounded from the brush as Finch took aim. His hands trembled, heart pounding violently against his chest. With a heavy breath, he grinned.

"I've got you..."

The lantern that hung from the porch burned dim when Finch arrived home. The sun had finally set upon Bridestowe, bringing with it the brutal winter chill. He staggered as he walked, and from a distance in the faint light, Elizabeth could make out the blood that soaked his clothing. In his grasp was a carcass. At first, she remained still on the porch, until her husband drew nearer. It was only then that she realized the body in his arms wasn't that of an animal.

Throwing a hand over her mouth to silence her gasped cry of shock, Elizabeth hurried towards her husband frantically. "Edward!"

The boy had been mutilated: torn at every limb, chest cut open and heart removed. The blood clung to his once fair hair, his mother sobbing over him as she ran her fingers through the tangled strands. She couldn't find words as he looked up at Finch. He stared off, silent. Vacant.

"What… what happened?" Elizabeth managed to choke out.

Finch didn't answer her. He only continued to stare into the distance, eyes flickering in the light of the lantern. Elizabeth trembled yet again as she looked him over, spotting the hunting knife strapped to his waist. The blood upon the blade glistened. She tensed as she held her breath, hearing a chuckle from Finch as he finally turned to her. Reaching down, he took hold of her chin, drawing her face up to look at him. She could feel the blood upon his hand spreading across her cheeks as the tears built in her eyes. A smile spread across his lips. In a hushed whisper, he chuckled.

"I killed the beast…"

Flat Line

Published in Spill Yr Guts Horror Zine (2018)

Bright lights surround me—endless walls of white, bleached of any trace of life. The metallic coldness stings beneath me, but I can feel the warm pricking at my skin from above. From those bright lights. My eyes waver opened and closed, and the voices around me are frantic. I can see the shadows—figures—but I can't make out their faces. The light is too bright. Slowly, I slip back into sleep.

There's darkness pricking at the corners of my vision, endless black I've yet to awaken from. Yet, behind closed eyes I see the colors, vibrant memories playing out before me. The warmth returns to me as I wander through the desolate dreams, slideshows painting the walls of my mind. Birthday parties, summer holidays, cozy nights by the fireplace. I never realized how beautiful these moments were—how long I'd neglected to cherish them.

There's a shaft of light streaming in before me, and I can make out two figures standing within. I'm hesitant at first, unsure of those who wait ahead, but as the light begins to dim, I can make out their features: a man and a woman. Father and Mother.

A smile stretches across my lips and I can't help but run towards them. The ground beneath me is uneasy, but I keep pushing on. I call out their names, beckoning them near, but they don't move. Still as statues they remain, looming in the distance as the light sets behind them, casting their shadows out upon me.

The darkness is closing in again.

Once more I call out to them, but my legs tremble with each step I take, a burning pain rushing up through them. From the waist down, my body stings—twinging in and out of being numb and in utter agony. I wince as I look back towards my parents, towards the light, but there's nothing left. They're slipping farther and farther away. Into the blackness. No, into the light. I fall to my knees and weep at the pain, holding tight to my calves as the throbbing pulses through me.

Make it stop… make it stop…

It's cold again, and the metallic chill rushes through me. Deep in my veins, I feel it creeping in. Dripping. One drop at a time. I hold myself, yearning for warmth, but it never comes. Just the frozen feeling of emptiness. Solitude. Isolation. And the pain… My lower extremities go numb.

I can hear voices around me once more, fewer than before. I can hear them whispering my name. There are tears in the words spoken. Hidden behind the sounds of machinery—the rhythmic beeps that seem to echo the pulsation of my heart. I place a hand against my chest, feeling each beat, listening to the mechanic resonance—waiting for the flat line. But it doesn't come.

"I'm afraid we see no hope of the boy coming out of it." One of the voices is clear now, and the harshness of his tone causes me to tremble.

The cries grow louder now, and I make out that they are from a woman *Mother*! I try to move, but the numbness in my legs keeps me planted where I kneel. I need to get to her. Need to hold her and let her know I'm alright. I can't stand to hear her cry.

"It's your decision," the voice states again, gruff and sincere. "His body is as good as dead as it is. While his mind may wander, if he never wakes up… Is that truly living? What I'm asking is, can the both of you handle it?"

My blood goes cold as I listen to the words, throat aching as I try to speak out. I need them to hear me. They *have* to hear me! I open my mouth but I'm lost for sound. Nothing comes from within—not even a small gasp of air, straining to be heard. Nothing.

Then, I hear my father.

"We'll do it…"

I want the light to return. I'm praying and hoping I could see it again—just once. For my eyes to open and my mind to be set free. I want to see them once more, feel the warmth of unmedicated blood pulsing through my veins. I want to hold Mother and tell her I love her. Tell Father I'm sorry. Hold them close. I want to speak. Just let me speak!

I use all the energy I have to attempt to stand. My knees tremble and I feel the muscles tearing as I cringe in agony. It's unbearable, but I have to stand. I must. They have to see. They have to!

The dripping in my veins seems to cease and the mechanical sounds around me die out. All that's left is the steady beeping, the echo of my heart, beating violently against my chest. Listen! Please listen!

I drag myself towards where the silhouettes of my parents once stood, yearning the faint shaft of light that mocks me. I hold out my hand, shaking, and part my lips once more. A weak, rusty sound awakens from deep within my throat and I manage to cry out.

"Father! Mother! I'm not really dead!"

There's silence.

"Please! I'm not dead..." My eyes fill with tears as my heart starts to slow. "I'm not..."

I hear the flat line.

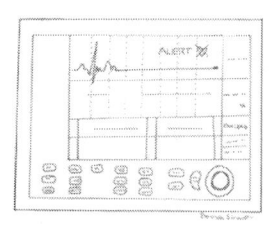

Sirena

Published in Riggwelter Press (2019)

I remember when we'd swim in the starlit waters. At sunset, we'd watch the ships dock for the night, sailors retreating to taverns for a mug of ale and a room. You told me you'd be departing with them someday—when the merchant ships returned from the foreign lands. I always told myself that you were but a dreamer. Casting your lines to the sea of stars. But when your ship did dock, you packed your bags and kissed my cheek, sails steadfast to the wind.

"I'd take you with me, but everyone knows a woman's bad luck on the sea."

Bad luck? I'd spent my life growing up along the shore, assisting my father—a poor fisherman—with his work. Countless times I'd sailed off in the bay, only twice never catching a net's worth. I remember telling you that, how I, too, longed for adventure on the sea—to see exotic lands and treasures only the traders laid eyes on. That was my dream, the dream you said was too far-fetched to be real.

I pled you take me with you, even if I were to be smuggled. I wouldn't eat much, I swore. I was of a tiny build anyway and knew a life of poverty—fighting for a scrap of bread on the table each day. My begging went on for a while, and finally you gave in. I knew a part of you didn't want to leave me.

"You'll need a disguise," you said. "Something to keep the other sailors from becoming suspicious."

So you gathered up one of your biggest overcoats and a cap, and fixed me up just right. You wound my hair and tucked it up, careful no strands would hang down. And you bound my breasts just tight enough that no one would suspect a thing. You said you'd tell them I was your son—eager to see the seas. And I told you that'd be just alright. As long as we're together.

The men on board fell for our trick, and I earned a place swabbing decks. They took me as the youngest of the bunch and wanted to work me into a man—but slowly, as you coaxed them. By day I'd endure my laboring tasks and by night, I'd watch the stars. They were beautiful—crystalline gems sparkling above, trapped in their own waves, hoping to not burn out.

I thought of the treasures that lay ahead, of the finest silks and pearls. A poor girl like me had never seen such splendor—only heard the stories from the merchants returning from months on their voyage. I wondered if diamonds really did shine like stars; the only difference was a diamond could never go out.

In the coming months, dread befell the ship. Many of the men had fallen ill and the food was becoming scarce. Molding bread and sea water were all we were left with—and no land had been in sight. One of the sailors cursed the map, claiming it was a work of witchcraft—that we'd been going in circles. The wind hadn't been on their side, they said. They said they all were to starve.

I did my best to try and reassure them that all would be well. We needed to keep pushing on and find land, wherever it be. Surely there would be a tavern at the harbor to find direction from—at least, that's how things were in Plymouth. Yet, they still cursed to the skies and declared witchcraft; something I hardly held faith in.

Yet, they confirmed it true when one of the men spotted me in my chambers. I'd been turning in for the night, unwinding my hair and letting my aching and bruised ribs breathe. He reported me to the captain, claiming I wasn't your son, but a witch—the one bringing the plague to the sailors. They stormed my cabin and dragged me to the deck—squirming. Their hands left deep bruises on my flesh and I begged them to understand. I wasn't an omen of misfortune!

"Woman's bad luck on the sea…"

They held me down and bound my hands and legs with the thickest rope they could find. They gagged me with old rags, silencing me, and carrying out their orders. You stood off to the side—watching—but you never said a word. Yet, somehow, I could hear in your thoughts the word *witch*. You believed them…

Without second thought, they tossed me overboard, giving their "misfortune" to the sea. I struggled against the waves, attempting to break free, but the rope was too tight and the water too deep. My lungs burned, aching for a breath, but it never came. And all I could see in my mind was you, standing there, without a word, watching me die. Watching me... *You never loved me.*

The ropes began to loosen and I could feel my legs begin to morph. Bound together, becoming one, like the sturdy tail of a whale. I managed to release my gag, fearful of taking a breath, but my lungs gave in and I inhaled—surprised by the welcoming feeling. The embrace.

    My body floated along, limp, but strong, marveled by the changes the sea had done. I was one with the waves, a being of the deep, and I accepted my fate.

    But still, I could feel you watching.

I remember when we'd swim in the starlit waters. Back then, I was of the land—with two legs standing proudly towards the sun. Towards my dreams. Now, the sea is my only companion. Filled with the salty taste of betrayal. *Your* betrayal.

    And I still wait, as I did years before, waiting for the merchant ships to dock for the night. Waiting, for the moonlight to grace the waters, illuminating even the darkest caverns below. The sharp rocky cliffs surrounding my haven remind me of those diamonds I once longed for. Sturdy, ever shining. *Immortal*. And it's with my voice I beckon them—calling them to the treasures they thought they desired. But when their vessels reach the mainland, they're met with nothing but destruction.

Greed is a killer.

I can't help but smile as I see them sink below—crying out for help as the waves devour them. If only they had embraced the sea and her wonders. If only they realized that she, too, gives back what she was given.

And still I wait. Wait for the ship I remember all those years before. Wait for the sailor who did me wrong. Turned against me and cast me away. My dear, we will swim the same waters once again—when your blood is illuminated within it like the stars.

Isolation

Published in Alcyone Magazine (2019)

I must be dreaming, you tell yourself again and again. If that's so, why haven't you awoken yet? You question yourself with this every day, puzzled with your surroundings and just how you arrived there. How uncanny it all is. So familiar, yet at the same time, so distant. You don't remember how you got here, and because of that, you fear you never will find your way out. All you can do is keep affirming; *I must be dreaming, I must be dreaming*. But, when will you wake up?

You remember the little things from before you arrived. Your name, where you're from, etc. None of them really matter anymore, at least not while you're here. But where is here? You know you've seen it before, once, somewhere. Perhaps it was the space in the back of your mind when you were alone, that space you longed to slip into to find peace in the world. Your isolation. Certainly that's what it feels like. You're all alone here, without memories and without affirmation. Your only companion has become your shadow, but even he, too, has fallen silent. Now, you only speak to yourself.

It's not that this place isn't beautiful. You described it once as being perfect; the place one could only call paradise. You said it was like your Garden of Eden, and maybe you were right. Perhaps you are returning to paradise and righteousness and a time simpler than the life you once led. The life you seem to have forgotten.

The grass is soft beneath you as you walk and it smells fresh and full of life. Endless meadows surround you, blossoming with delicate flowers while the sun beats down on your back. It warms you, but it's not scorching. It's perfect. Everything's perfect—at least, that's what you said. You gaze up to the skies above, at their deep hues of fuchsia and violet. That's the only thing that leads you to believe this is a dream. For in reality, isn't the sky blue?

You seem to forget about it after a while and lie down in the grass. There's a gentle breeze now and it makes the blades tickle your bare arms and legs as you stare up at the candy-colored sky. *I must be dreaming.* Slowly, through the warmth and tenderness of the grass blanketing you, the swirling of sun and sky send you into a trance. And thus, you find yourself dozing off.

You said you never cared much for your sister. Growing up, you complained she was the most favored because she was the first born. Although your parents treated you as equals, you still continued to defend your reasoning as to why you believed she was privileged. When they defended back, you only said, *that's because you baby me.*

But it was your sister that would end up babying you. When you had fallen sick from that terrible disease, left bedridden and barely able to move, she was by your side, assisting you with everything you needed. One would normally admire their sibling for doing such things, you'd tell yourself, but you resented it. All day and night, she would be at your bedside, asking if you needed anything. You'd simply tell her, *no*, and hope that from there, she would leave you in peace. That's what you needed. Peace. Quiet. Isolation.

Day after day, she would slip upstairs to your room with some warm soup, offering to help feed you if you weren't able. As always, you would nudge her away, proving that you still had the energy to care for yourself. When you finished, it was the same routine with her returning to gather your empty bowl before slipping your medication over to you. That bottle of small white pills mocked you from the day you were prescribed them; three times a day they'd be sent down your throat and make you resent your situation even more. That was what finally led you to hiding them after every meal. Your sister would never know. When she reappeared for the last time in the evening, collecting your medication bottle, she would ask if you needed anything as usual. Instead of saying no, this time, you would mutter, *I just want to be alone.*

For a while, she did begin to leave you be, until she discovered your untaken medication hidden in the drawer of your nightstand. After that, she would stand over you like an overseer, commanding you to take it. *It's the only way you'll get better*, she said. You, however, knew there was no way of getting "better". The medication was only a false hope which seemed to push the inevitable deathbed farther back. You already knew you were lying on it.

When your eyes finally open up, you realize you're still in your dreamscape. Nothing has changed here: the sun, the grass, the sky. It's all the way you left it before you closed your eyes. *If only reality were this simple…*

You begin walking again, further through the meadow. Again, you tell yourself that this all must be a dream—meadows don't go on forever, the sun can't always light up the sky. Yet, the feeling of dread still creeps up your back as you remind yourself that you had been sleeping. Dreaming. You carry on, pondering the possibilities. One usually fell asleep to dream of fantasy, you think, not to dream of reality.

The last thing you remember was falling asleep. After pushing your next dose of pills under your mattress so that your sister would suspect you took them (she got into a habit of checking your drawer once you dozed off), you were able to relax. The room slipped into a steady darkness and tiny specs of black overtook your vision. They usually only appeared when you stared at the ceiling for too long once the lights had been turned off for the night, or just before someone was about to faint. But, you didn't feel that strange light-headedness that often accompanied them. Instead, you felt at peace. The peace you said you longed for so many times before.

It was when you awoke that you realized you were here. There was sun for the first time, not the shadows your room was forced to remain in to help you rest. No longer were you trapped in your bed, but you could wander freely. Your room was now a meadow and there were no walls encasing it. There was no medication, no sister hovering over you, and no sickness. Each breath you took was full of life, fresh and sweet. It was as if you had been reborn, or at least that's what you said before you affirmed that you were dreaming.

You stop momentarily when you hear her voice brushing passed your ear, carried by the gentle breeze. It's quiet at first, but then picks up, shaking the blades of grass. You can't make out what she's saying, but you know it's your sister. You've heard her scold you enough growing up and now, with your medication. Yet, as much as you want to cringe at her voice, part of you longs to stay and listen. She is the first thing you have heard. The first breath of the living that was not your own. But where was she? You turn around and begin back towards where you came from, this time walking faster.

Although you say you never cared much for your sister, you know that's a lie. She may have been overbearing at times and dominated you growing up with her games, but in her big-sister control, you still loved her. She was the one you could turn to when your parents punished you for tracking mud through the house or breaking one of their drinking glasses. She was the one that you snuck out with after dark just so you could sit on the roof and watch the stars. She was the one who you could tell all your secrets, and know that your mother and father would never hear of them. You trusted her, even though you had grown to resent her.

    Maybe it wasn't her you resented, you think as you carry on. Maybe it was just the overbearing world and the people in it. Perhaps, just life itself was becoming too much.

    Your sister was there with you the day you were diagnosed. You can't remember any of the details, but you can still feel her hand tightly clutching yours as the doctor explained the risks, treatments, and your eventual outcome. You kept your head lowered through all this, teeth gritted together in a disbelieved rage. It wasn't your fault, you knew that. Everyone knew that. But, for some reason, you felt as if it were. That was when she took you home and put you to bed, promising to care for you in every way she could. She said there was a way you could get better, she swore there was, but you knew better than her that there was no way avoiding the "eventual outcome".

Had it not been for the deaths of your parents as they grew older, perhaps she wouldn't have been so paranoid. Your father passed away from a stroke and your mother died only a few months later from what your sister was certain was grief. You remember that her husband-to-be also broke it off with her after admitting he had been cheating a month before the wedding, and then begin to realize why her control over you had grown.

You stop short in the meadow again and let the breeze toss your hair.

She was just afraid of losing you, you think. Her consistent checking up on you was only to assure that you were still there, still breathing. Yet, you ushered her away. You wanted to be left alone. And now, *she* was alone; the very fear that she hoped would never come true.

No, you tell yourself, *it's not true. I must be dreaming.*

Her voice is clear now. When you finally stop to listen to her words, you feel the wind become colder. Steadily. It is then you realize she's not alone.

He wasn't taking his medication, she says. *I fear that's what pushed this to happen.*

Her voice is shaky and you can tell that she's crying. You can't make out the words of the person with her, but she soon answers back. This time, she's crying harder.

I tried so hard to protect him, so that it wouldn't come to this.

It was inevitable. For the first time, the voice of the other becomes clear to you. *We discussed the risks of his illness and regardless of if he took his medication or not, this was bound to happen.*

Your body doesn't know whether to tense up as you listen, or to remain at ease. You still aren't sure if what you're hearing is part of your dream or if voices are around you while you sleep. That's all it is, you keep assuring yourself. Sleep. Why couldn't she see that?

You try to call out to her, letting her know that you're here and safe. *This is all just a dream*, you explain, *I'll be waking up soon. Don't cry*! Yet, it's when her tears become harsher and you realize that each of your hollers to her fall silent that you start to understand. You haven't woken up. You've never woken up. Not even after falling asleep.

There were times in the meadow where you had dozed off, listening to the breeze through the blades of grass as the gentle lullaby of nature was hummed. The warmth of the sun provided an extra blanket as you partook in your slumber. It was peaceful, yes, exactly what you once had wanted; but when you awoke, you were still trapped within the dream. What did you really wake up from? Your dreams here were nothing more than reality, glimpses of the past and memories you thought to have forgotten. It was the reality which was now the dream.

The wind begins to pick up again as the sun steadily sets in the distance. You cry out to her again, begging that she'll hear you. *I'm here! I'm here!* Your voice has become like your shadow now—silent. As the sky above is drained of its once vibrant hues, becoming dull and grey, even her voice fades for you. Only glimpses of words come through now, spiraling on the harsh gusts around you.

Comatose...Promised... Help... Inevitable... Love... Sorry...

For the first time in your dreamland, rain begins to fall from the sky. It's cold to the touch, nothing like the once warm sun had been. The voices are gone now, only the rain resonating off the ground. The grass beneath your feet sags into the rising mud, and your cries become drowned out once more. The winds had taken your voice with that of your sister.

Isolation was what you always dreamed of, but now it has become your reality. Even when the sun begins to rise, drying the wet blades of grass and flowers of the meadow, you understand this. Though peace is beautiful, part of you longs for your sister's voice once again; for your bed, your medication. Your life built around lies and false hope, but also around love.

Never before did the sun here feel so cold.

You don't tell yourself that you must be dreaming anymore. You know the truth now and trying to affirm it only causes you more dread. Things go back to how they were here again; serine and silent. You talk to your shadow in hopes that he'll answer, but just like last time, he never does. Not even the grass sings anymore, you realize. Everything is too quiet. Too perfect. *But, you think as you sit alone in the middle of that meadow, it's no longer perfect for me.*

No, you don't tell yourself you must be dreaming. In fact, dreams no longer are what you are trying to escape from. It's reality—the cruel reality of your coma. It's the dreams you hold on to. For only in dreams, you find your reality; your *real* reality. And now, you can't help but wish to never wake up.

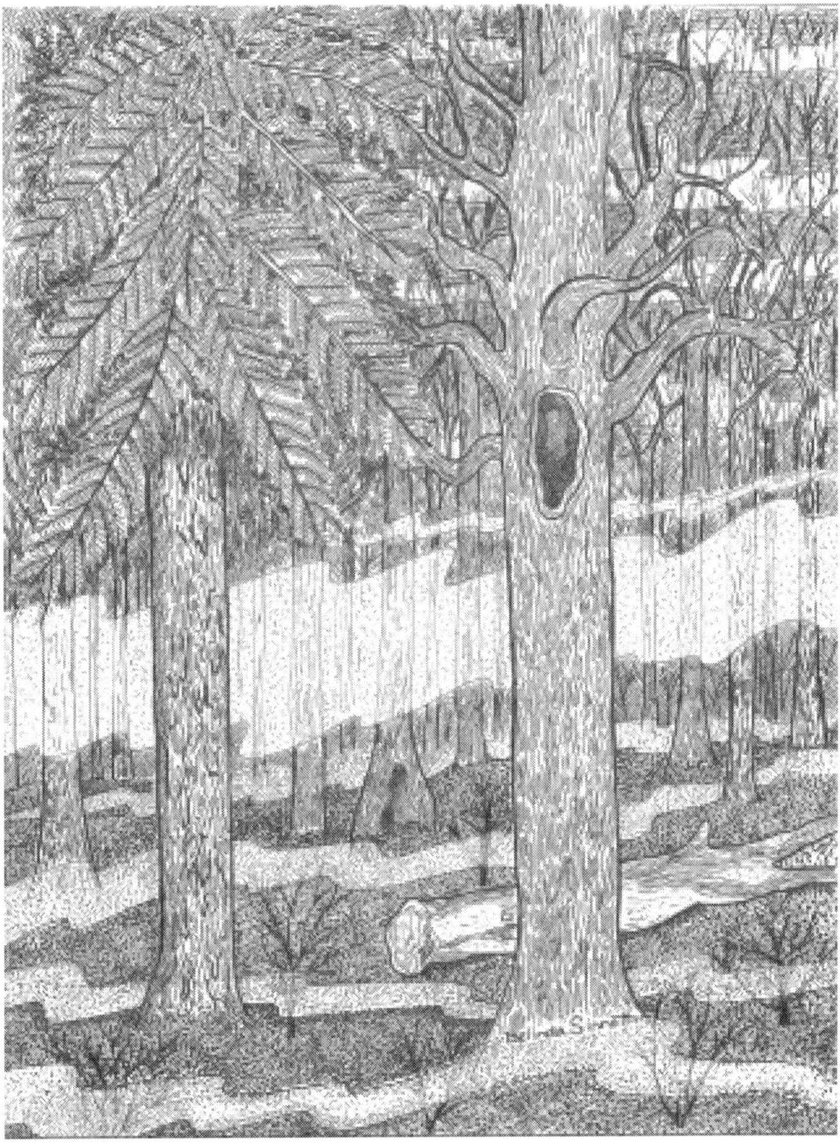

Beyond the Pines

Published in Spill Yr Guts Horror Zine (2019)

A labyrinth of trees were all they came to know. But yet, the branches that covered the orphanage windows were nothing in comparison to the endless forest surrounding them. The last few leaves of the year let in the only light that trickled down from above, but the rest of the woodland was shrouded in shadow. And silence. The only sound that would rise up, deep in the night, was from beyond the pines. An ancient, long-forgotten spirit who promised blood for freedom.

Enoch, the eldest, denied such a thought. Freedom from the forest would come from wit—instinct. But as the days grew longer and blended together, he soon began to realize that perhaps the spirit was right. Perhaps, the only way to free themselves from the long, lost paths was to give in. Give in to the shadows, give in to the forest, and give in to Death.

Death was no stranger in the maze of trees. Though winter made him weak, the inhabitants of the forest knew better. He was hungrier than ever when the snow blanketed the earth, leaving no source of life for him to feast upon. Animals took to their dens to hibernate until spring, and he would only be able to leech from the few passersby. But the forest saw no visitors this season, and Death was beginning to starve. That is, of course, until Enoch and Acorn came along.

Acorn scuffed his feet through the fallen leaves and thin layer of snow that coated the ground. His hands were shoved deep into his pockets to try and keep warm, but the dropping temperature made it harder. The orphanage only had a small supply of winter clothes to begin with, and his secondhand coat certainly didn't do as suffice a job as it could. Noticing his brother had been falling behind, Enoch stopped.

"Can't you go any faster? It's getting colder out here," he jabbed. "I told you we shouldn't have played out here. I *told* you we should have stayed put. It's your fault we're lost. And it's not going to be your fault we catch our death."

"I'm sorry, Enoch…"

Acorn kept his head and voice low, picking up his pace only slightly. Being exposed to the elements the past few days with no real means of warmth had been taking its toll on him—on *both* of them. He could feel the fever starting to rise and his occasional coughs had become more frequent.

But it wasn't just the coldness from the air he'd been feeling ill from. He'd seen so much change in his brother since they became known to the forest. His tone being the main thing. Enoch was always so soft spoken and caring—but lately, in the week or so they had been wandering aimlessly through the wood, he became bitter. He had been full of hope and promises to Acorn—playing the role as his father when he needed it—but now, there was nothing left in his words but anger and defeat.

"D-do you think anyone is looking for us, Enoch?" Acorn asked once he was at his brother's side.

"*Us*? Highly unlikely. I doubt they've even noticed we've gone missing," Enoch said. "Face it, kid. We don't have anyone who misses us. We're stray dogs are far as they're concerned. One less... erm... *two* less mouths to feed."

Enoch looked up to the canopy of branches that hung above them. A few flakes of snow began to fall from the greying skies. He sighed.

"No one is looking for us, James."

Acorn flinched. He hadn't heard his name, *James*, spoken in so long. Enoch had always called him "Acorn", for as long as he could remember. *You're like a little acorn, falling not too far from the tree.* Although five years apart, the two were inseparable. Mainly, Acorn from Enoch, but even just the same. The younger wanted nothing more than to be just like his big brother. And so, the name stuck. Only their mother and father had used "James"—and even then, it was only to be formal. But since their passing, he rarely heard it. Not even from the caregivers at the orphanage.

That was another thing, Acorn told himself, that was lost to the wood.

"Now let's keep moving. We can't be too far from the main road now. Or, at least a town or something."

Enoch started ahead once more, leaving Acorn standing on the path as the snow continued to fall. It took him a moment before he, too, sighed, and followed along behind his brother.

The shadows of night fell deep upon the clearing where the brothers stayed the night. They huddled close together, using their bodies as warmth. The snow had died down, but it didn't keep the cold from creeping in. The temperatures of night were far lower than day. And Death prowled the forest with craving.

It was Enoch who heard the voice first—slipping in through his dreams.

Why do you keep holding on to hope, dear boy? You've said it yourself—no one is looking for you.

"I made a promise to my brother," Enoch stated firmly. "I swore to him I'd get him home, and that's what I'm going to do."

Home? Enoch could hear the grin in Death's voice. *But, you have no home. Only that bleak, empty orphanage to go back to. Is that what you want?*

"That's one step closer to home than here."

Enoch searched around himself, seeking out the voice. But all he saw was trees. Endless, branching trees. And shadow.

"Why don't you show yourself? Are you afraid?"

Fear is a feeling created by the one it haunts. It does not have a physical form. I am much like fear. I am very real—but only become more prominent as you allow it.

"Then I ask you to leave. You're only slowing us down."

Such a large favor from a small soul. Surely you know why I'm here.

The cold wind picked up from the west, stinging Enoch's cheek. He turned his face away from the gust, only to notice Acorn sound asleep.

You're both getting sick—exposure to the elements. Winter is eating away at you with your hunger. It won't be long until you're begging for me, not pushing me away.

"No," Enoch said. "We're not giving in to you. We're going home, and that's that. I made a promise to James…"

And you can fulfill that promise. Give your brother to me, and I'll set him free. I'll send him home.

Enoch was taken back. "What!?"

Face it, child… home is a lifetime away. It's a vision you two have built up and hoped for, but it will never come. How many years will you sit in that orphanage and wait? How many more days can your brother hold out without food? Warmth?

Enoch heard a deep, wet cough from Acorn.

I only offer freedom. And the price is so little. Let me take the burden off your hands and you'll be free. You'll both be free.

"I-I can't…"

I promised you freedom, did I not? I can take you home. All it costs is your brother. And he, too, will be free.

The dripping of snow melting from the trees is what awoke Enoch that morning. He sat up, head spinning from his dreams, and the sickness that had crept upon him. He coughed once, heavy, feeling the phlegm cling in his throat. And it hurt to breathe—how *much* it hurt to breathe. He glanced over at Acorn, still sound asleep in the snow. His cheeks were pale, lined only with the rosiness of the cold that nipped him.

"J-James…?"

There was no response. Enoch scooted closer to him, resting a hand against his brother's forehead. He was expecting it to be warm, from the fever he knew had been breaking, but he was cold. So, very cold. Enoch tried to catch a whimpering breath, but it only got caught in his lungs and stung. The tears came naturally, though.

"E-Enoch…?"

Enoch looked back to his brother, the boy's eyes just barely open.

"I-It's so cold. And I'm so tired… I want to go home."

The wind began to blow harder as Enoch felt the tears coming again.

"How much farther…?"

"Not much," Enoch whispered. "Not much…"

When evening fell, Enoch was barely walking. The cold took to him as the snow around his feet grew deeper. In his arms, he carried Acorn. When he reached the thickest part of the forest, where the branches twisted themselves in hellish form, Enoch fell to his knees.

Have you brought me what I asked for?

Enoch looked for the voice beyond the trees, but there was nothing but darkness. With trembling arms, he moved Acorn from against his chest and into the snow. A thick stain of blood coated the front of his coat, and in a smooth line across the boy's neck. It was the only thing that had kept him warm.

"I did what you asked…," Enoch spoke softly, voice caught in the lump in his throat. "Now take us home."

For the first time, there was no response from Death. The trees seemed to vibrate from a hollow chuckle, but soon, it was overtaken by just the wind. The snow began to fall heavy once again, covering Acorn's body as Enoch cried out.

"You promised! You promised you'd take us home!"

Silence was all that met Enoch. He couldn't stop the tears as he rested a hand upon his brother's forehead once more.

I promised you freedom. The voice softly drifted in. *You're free of the burden your brother put on you. Isn't that what you wanted?*

A sharp twinge was sent through Enoch's chest at the words. Surely he had thought here and there that life without Acorn would be simpler. That not worrying about looking after him, not worrying about finding a home they could go to together, would make life simpler. Easier. But no matter how much he often wished that fantasy true, he knew the reality of it.

Acorn needed him. And he knew that deep down, he needed Acorn, too.

"I wanted to go home… To bring Acorn home!"

But silly boy… you were home. So long as you had each other.

Enoch felt the cold breath of Death on the wind.

But now? You are lost. Lost forever to the trees and the burden of loneliness. And now, that loneliness will be the only home you know.

The wind died down, and the heavy feeling of Death began to fade. Enoch pulled Acorn close, burying his face into his brother's hair as he tried to hold back the tears. Around him, there was nothing but silence and the open, endless forest.

As the snowflakes fell from the grey skies above, the last of the season's dying leaves broke free of the safety of its branch. It floated down on the cold winter wind, landing not too far from the trunk of its tree. But soon, it was forgotten under the steadily rising snow.

The Hunger

Published in Disturbed Digest (2019)

It started with the hunger. Deep, gnawing pain that couldn't be satisfied. And the more I consumed, the hungrier I became.

The winter had been long and cold, nor'easters blowing in and covering the land in deep snow. Travel to town was nearly impossible in the foot or so that would pile up with each storm, and the forest behind my cabin seemed to only grow darker as the snow rose. It wasn't long before the cans and preserves I had rationed over the spring became a necessity, and hunting my only source of meat. But even then, most of the wildlife had taken cover. And thus, hunts were often failed attempts.

But, it was that hunt in particular that I came across fresh meat.

My dog tracked it first, howling over the bloody remains. He sniffed it over, tail wagging lowly as I approached. The snow had kept what was left of the carcass well preserved, and from the look of the supply, it had only been a few hours. Hunting at daybreak became the norm, in hopes of catching unsuspecting prey as they awoke. And whatever I had stumbled upon had made the wrong choice of leaving the safety of its slumber before sunrise. Though most of what was left had been dragged off, there was still plenty to take. From the size of the animal, my guess was that it had been a small deer. I used my hunting knife to cut away what I could of the flesh. Once I had a decent amount, I headed back to the cabin. There would be enough to last another day or two with the stock I'd taken. And the less I had to venture out into the elements, the better.

There seemed to be no end to the snow.

I cooked the meat all day into evening, combining it with spices and the few vegetables left from before winter's worst had struck. It was a good, smooth, tender chunk—one of the best pieces of meat I'd had. The change in having a warm meal filled me, as canned goods were the only source of nutrition I had come by in recent weeks. I'd offered some of it to my dog, but he simply whined in disapproval. Surely he had been hungry. There had been far less for him to eat than me—and what few table scraps he had been being given weren't enough to survive on. But, I gave up on insisting and finished the rest for myself.

When the fireplace embers died down, I retired to bed. The early nights and the cold air brought nothing but exhaustion, and beneath the covers became the best place to escape them.

It didn't take long to fall asleep with a fulfilled appetite, but there was something about that night which lingered. My room seemed darker than usual, and the tree branches beside my window cast long, bony shadows across the floor in the light of the moon. From the forest, beyond the trees, I swore I could hear someone calling—whispering—my name. But the howls of the wind drowned it out, and convinced me it was only winter beckoning the night. And thus, I fell into slumber, letting the shadows engulf me.

At first, I thought the figure standing before me was a deer. But when I saw through the darkness in the milk light of moon, I saw that no deer it was. It stood on two legs, antlers rising from its skull like the branches of the old birch trees of the forest. Hanging from them appeared to be flesh, perhaps from shedding their velvet layers. But there was blood amongst it, too. Where the face of the deer should have been was nothing but white bone, and the hollows of its eyes burned a deep yellow. At first, I thought they had caught the light of the moon—but their voids were too endless. And its teeth… The flat, grazing, herbivores that should have lined the jaws were nonexistent. Instead, they were long and sharp fangs, dripping with the same blood that coated the antlers. A foul stench of rotten flesh lingered in the air, and with each hissy breath the creature emitted, the more I could smell it. It stood at the foot of my bed, eying me through the shadows.

Nathaniel…

The whisper I had sworn was from the winds pricked at my ears again. Only this time, I knew it was coming from before me. At the edge of my bed. The yellow eyes of the beast began to flicker like the embers of my fireplace just hours before. The odor was growing stronger, burning at my nostrils. It was becoming unbearable.

Nathaniel...

This time, there was more force in the guttural breath. I felt it brush against my face in a warm, heavy blow. Outside, the light of the moon bathed the forest, the trees appearing to rise from a white, glowing abyss. My room spun from the brightness and the smell, and the hot breath against my skin. The beast spoke again, no longer in a whisper.

He who eats the flesh becomes the beast!

The nightmares had been a daily occurrence after that night. All so heavily vivid. I'd convinced myself there was no creature in my room, and that only the trick of the light and shadows had created it. During the day, I continued on as I had, hunting early in the morning and venturing home before the snow grew deeper by noon. There still was little to catch in the forest, but the occasional rabbit was enough for a warm meal.

Yet, just as the nightmares had grown with each setting of the sun, so did my hunger. It started out gradual—the discomfort of having missed a meal gurgling through my stomach. But as the days passed, that discomfort turned into pain. Deep, aggravating pain in the pit of my being. I'd gone through cans of preserves without a single bit of satisfaction, and the vegetables... and the meat. It had gotten to the point I was consuming it raw. Fresh from the hunt. I didn't bother skinning the prey anymore. I'd sit there in the snow, tearing through the warm flesh, first with my knife, and then with my teeth.

But it didn't quell the pains.

Hunger overtook me and in the matter of a week, I could see my bones beginning to show beneath my skin. There was no way, I was convinced, one could lose weight so quickly. And that night, I consumed all that was left in my cellar, salvaged for spring.

I lay in the moonlight that drenched my bedroom floor, trembling from the gnawing that ate away at my insides. There was no food left. I'd eaten all that was stored away in a matter of days—*hours*! And yet, I still craved food.

No. *Flesh*.

But the rabbits weren't satisfying enough anymore, and the deer were too hard to track down. They could hear me move in the snow, and they avoided my presence. That and the smell… I'd tried to bathe it off me, but as each day passed, I got a whiff of that heavy, rotting stench from my dreams. Only this time, it was coming from me. I knew for certain if an animal picked up my scent, they'd be long gone. Not even my *dog* could bear being around me. And that was when I knew I was dying.

The starvation had gotten to me. The hunger and the cold of winter. I was wasting away to a bag of bones, and the smell I had been emitting was my insides dying. Death slowly making its way from the inside out. But I had been eating. I'd eaten more than I ever had. But still, it wasn't enough.

It was the meat... That's all I could tell myself. There must have been something wrong with the meat. The flesh. It seemed so well preserved in the snow, but I should have known better. Parasites, I thought, some sort of disease inhabiting it. And I had consumed it all. Every last piece I brought home. And now, I was becoming nothing more than the sorry carcass left to rot in the forest. Now, it was *me* who was rotting.

The creature appeared in my dreams that night again, whispering my name and taunting me with its vile words. And its eyes continued to burn those deep, yellow embers. Mocking me. Mocking the withering corpse I was becoming.

Nathaniel...

My strength had been so little, I couldn't attempt to ward it off. Cast it out of my home and back to the forest I knew it had slunk from. From outside my door, I could hear my dog whimpering, pawing to get in. I was certain he had sensed my distress. My frail, dying body hallucinating such a horrific being. But I couldn't wake up. Not the fear or the eventual barking beyond the door would stir me.

Nathaniel...

All I could do was wait for the sun. Or death. Whichever chose to come first.

You need to eat...

My body lay slouched in the doorway that next morning. It was the farthest I could make it. My legs had no strength left and I could barely keep my head raised. The burning in my stomach had spread through my body, and the pain was too much to bear.

The monster was right. I needed to eat. But there was nothing left. And I was far too weak to attempt to track something down in the forest. The rabbits feared me as I feared the beast. Feared *death*. I was no match in trying to catch them at this point.

As the pain continued to eat away at my insides, I listened to the quiet whimpering of my dog down the hall. The hunger must have been getting to him, too. He hadn't eaten when I had—he refused the meat that night. And, I thought to myself, he probably smelled the sickness it was tainted with. He was the wise one. But now, we both were suffering for it.

His whines grew louder and it wasn't long before I couldn't bear it. Between that and the sounds of my stomach digesting itself, it was making me nauseous. And there was nothing left in me to even vomit at this point.

You need to eat...

The monster's words ate away at my thoughts. I knew he was right. With trembling hands, I removed my hunting knife from its sheath. It was still coated in a thin layer of blood from the last hunt. I held the blade close to me and gave in to the words.

You need to eat...

I gathered what strength I had and made my way down the hall.

Silence overtook the house that night, aside from the crackling fire that cooked the fresh meat. I stared into the flickering flames with cavernous craving. My head spun, and the aches that were once in my pit now seemed to rise to my temple. I was losing focus. The hunger was now causing me to become lightheaded. And the more I gazed into the fire, the more I felt the heaviness seep through my skull.

When the meat was finished, I ravenously devoured it. It was all that was left. It was all that *would* be left. But even then, even after consuming all that was left in the pot, I still wanted more. It hadn't satisfied even the smallest of my pains. And now, there was nothing.

Tears pricked at the corners of my eyes, and it hurt as they began to roll down my cheeks. The pressure in my head was becoming sharper, but all it managed was to get more tears from me. I knew this was it. I had no strength to venture into the forest. Not alone. And now, all there was to do was just sit. Sit and wait.

Death would be coming soon. That, I was sure of.

When the pain in my head didn't subside by morning, I took to the bathroom to find any source of medication that could ease the pain. I knew on an empty stomach, it wasn't a safe choice—but the throbbing aches in my head were becoming more unbearable than those in my stomach. I found a bottle of aspirin in the medicine cabinet and stared at the label reluctantly. I could just devour the bottle—perhaps the pain would subside and the hunger would end. That, or it could encourage death to hurry. Either way, I thought, at this point, there was nothing to lose.

Shutting the cabinet, I glanced into the mirror above the sink only for a second, but that was long enough for my eyes to catch the short, nobs that were sprouting from my skull. I was taken aback as I ran my fingers along them, wincing as even the slightest touch sent a sharp pressure through my head. I could feel the warm, sticky blood that bubbled beneath them clinging to my fingers. They'd torn right through my scalp, as if they were part of my skull itself. They were hard—definitely bone. And even though they were small, that didn't shake the terror of what was overtaking me.

It was the monster. He had been right.

I looked back to the mirror and in place of my reflection, there he was. The creature that had been haunting my dreams. Driving me to madness—starving what little slumber I managed to get. His eyes didn't glow in the light of my bathroom. Instead, they were dark, endless voids hollowed out in his skull. The blood still painted his teeth; and now that I saw him in vivid light, I knew the flesh that hung from his antlers wasn't his own. In fact, it wasn't animal at all. It was *human*.

He who eats the flesh becomes the beast…

A gust of wind and snow from the storm howled outside, and the lights in the house went out.

By the third day, the nubs had grown twice in size, and it was harder to lift my head than before. There was no more pain in my stomach—now it was just a hollow, empty feeling. There was nothing left for the agony to feast on. I lay in the darkness of my bedroom, on the hard floor, letting the shadows tease me with their branching arms. I prayed it would be the beast. He hadn't showed himself since the day in the mirror. But I was ready. He was death. I knew that's what he was. And I was *ready*.

But when he did come, it was only in the form of the trees. I saw his form amidst the shadows on the wall, and I could hear him speak in his low, gravely whisper.

Nathaniel…

There was the pain again. A quick, sharp twinge in my abdomen. The hunger was returning.

With what strength I had, I watched the silhouettes of the creature dance across the walls and floor. Stretching as the light of the moon bathed more and more of the room.

You must eat, Nathaniel. You must eat…

But there was nothing left. I knew it would only be a matter of time before I gave in to the hunger and searched the forest once more. I knew I wouldn't return. Either the frigid cold or the starvation would claim me. But, it was becoming a risk I was willing to take. After all, I reminded myself, at least searching meant trying to survive. Staying here meant certain death. Perhaps in the morning I would attempt to venture out once more.

Only with flesh will you grow stronger, Nathaniel...

The beast's words echoed through the room. With them, I could feel his warm breath once again. It caressed my skin, tightening itself around my being.

You must eat.

You must eat.

I felt myself wavering in and out of consciousness. The shadows around me spun and the room grew darker. The voice faded the deeper under I fell.

The flesh...

You must.

Eat the flesh...

You must.

Become the beast...

At daybreak, I gathered my energy to do what I had done weeks before when the snow first began to fall. I layered myself in long sleeves and coats, and doubled up a pair of gloves. With how little was left on my bones, I knew the temperatures would be colder than normal. And I knew it wouldn't be long before the frost ate away at what was left of me, and I would become the next carcass well preserved in the woods. Left to the elements.

I worked to secure a wool hat upon my head, but it was difficult with the ever-growing antlers. I managed to cover them as best I could, before strapping my hunting knife to me. The snow was deep, but I prayed there would be something out there. Something I could find for just one meal. I had to eat…

As I trudged through the snow that blanketed my property, I stopped at the far end of my gate. The forest loomed over me to the right—dark trees and wildlife I knew hid within them. To the left was the center of town. The long trek back to the shops and markets I had no intention of returning to until spring. The road hadn't been plowed, as I had predicted, and the steadily rising winter wind reminded me of just how cold and hungry I was.

I stood at the gate for only a moment longer before buttoning my coat. With a guttural sigh, I turned my back to the forest.

"I must eat…" I whispered.

The village wasn't that far, I thought. If I found the strength, I could make it. After all, there was plenty to eat there. And far more fresh flesh to satisfy the hunger.

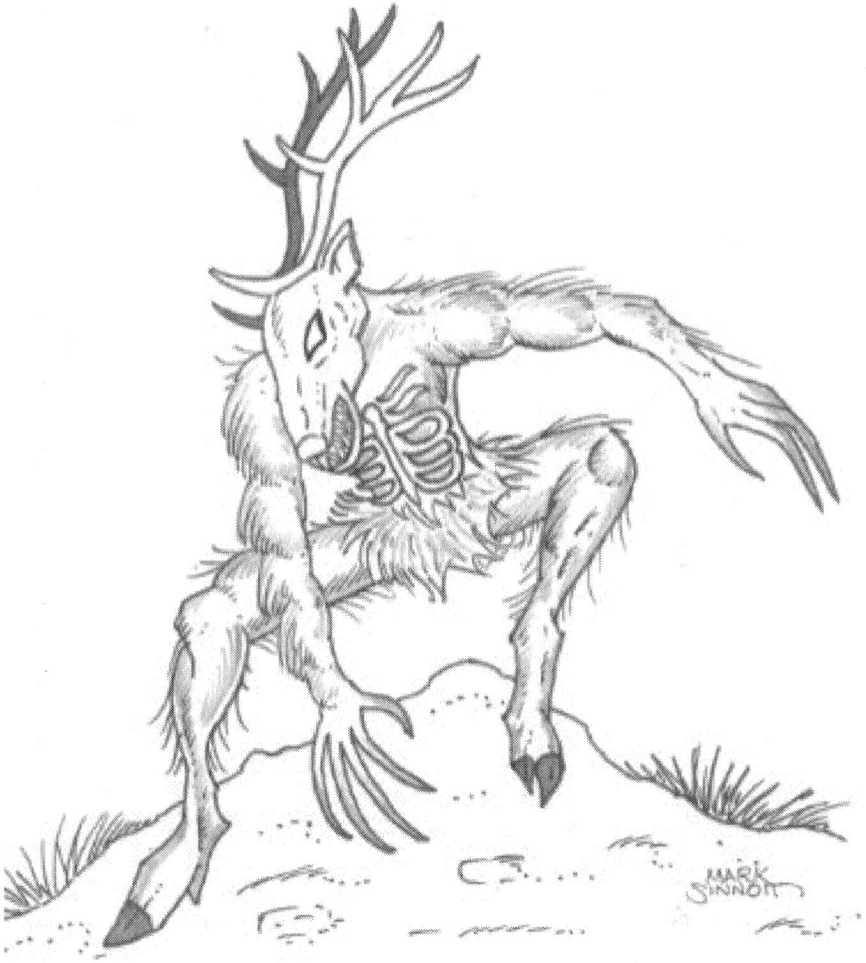
MARK SINNOTT

A Place of His Own

Published in Black Petals Magazine (2019)

There's something ominous about railroads. In the light of day, they're nothing more than a busy route, transporting goods and people through the countryside. Onlookers line the rails, waving as each carrier car rattles by. This continues until sunset, until the last train makes its way through the fields, and silence overtakes the land. But at night, when the tracks go still, whispers can be heard rising from beneath the framework. Stories of lies, betrayal, and deceit. Revenge. The people of Petersburg have come to know these stories well, and heed their warnings.

The Winchester family wouldn't have it any other way.

At the turn of the century, Robert Winchester had bought up most of the stocks in the Beeding and Petersburg railroads. Within only a few years, he was sitting on a gold mine—a gold mine he knew would last his family generations. Newly wed and in need of a home where he and his wife, Mary, planned to raise a family, Robert had an estate built in the middle of the Petersburg village. While only he and his wife took up residence in the house, it was large enough for multiple families to make use of the living space. And that's why, at Mary Winchester's request, her brother Jacob moved in.

Mary and Jacob always had a close relationship. The two would spend time together whenever they could, laughing over tea and good books—or the stocks. More money was falling into their laps as the rails expanded across the country, and people from up north began to head west. Robert, with the new wealth that continued to pour in, decided to build a home at the far end of the property. Although smaller than the main house on the estate, a good two or three families could still reside within and have enough room to barely come in contact if desired. Robert suggested Jacob move in once it was finished—a place of his own. But Mary objected. She wouldn't have Jacob, her dear brother, taken from her. Even if it was simply across the property. And so, the newly built home became the servants' house. And Jacob remained with Mary.

Petersburg is a small town, surrounded by endless fields of northeastern corn. With nowhere to go and not much to do, gossip and rumors are quick to spread. Through the fields, through the village, and through the church—where all the locals attended each and every Sunday. When Mary Winchester began to show that she was with child, the rumors became louder.

"I hear she's been sleeping with her brother. Her *own* brother!"

"The child isn't Robert's… The poor man doesn't know, though."

"How could a man be so blind? In his *own* home!"

Robert overheard the rumors once or twice, but he wouldn't believe it. Mary was faithful to him. And she assured him that the child was his.

In late October, Isaac Winchester was born. Isaac grew up with unconditional love from his mother, father, and uncle. He was taught the finer things in life—raised with the belief that he and his family were privileged beyond their wealth, and that one day, the stocks, the railroad, and the estate would all belong to him.

This, of course changed, when Robert decided to adopt when Isaac turned 15.

Mary no longer could bear children. Her pregnancy with Isaac had been complicated and since then, no matter what they tried, nothing worked. Robert had always dreamed of a large family, a multitude of heirs to continue the family name. While the blood line would eventually die out, he believed that the name itself was something worth living on. *And besides*, he would assure himself, *Isaac is of my own blood*. His linage would be more than enough.

And so, newly adopted William and Peter were given the Winchester name. Biological brothers, six years apart, the two of them had a close bond that was inseparable—much like Mary and Jacob's, Robert had noted. Perhaps that was why he was so drawn to them.

William was around the same age as Isaac, which put strain on the talk of inheritance. Robert mentioned giving half the shares promised to Isaac to William, causing competition. Yet, despite their indifference of each other, the two grew to tolerate one another—for the sake of their father. Peter, on the other hand, won deep love from Isaac. The two developed a bond as if they were brothers-by-blood—much to William's distaste. But he tried not to let it show. It was the least he could do to show he was grateful for the Winchesters welcoming the two of them in.

The tolerance in the family lasted for quite a few years, until Mary fell ill. As she lay dying, she asked that she speak to her husband in privacy, stating that he needed to know something before she passed. Robert was never the same after that day. He became distant and cold, and when Mary finally did succumb, he took to the parlor for the majority of his days. The stocks and railroad seemed to no longer interest him—and he never brought it up to his sons again. Until when, a few months later, he, too, passed away.

The Winchester will was supposed to divide the estate amongst the three brothers. Isaac and William sharing the majority of the stocks, and Peter getting just enough to build upon as he grew older. However, that wasn't what Robert left to the boys.

William earned his share of stocks, as did Peter, but Isaac was nowhere to be found. This baffled and upset him, as he was heir to the Winchester estate—by blood—and he knew he had seen the will initially when his father created it. But now, he had been stricken from it. Without warning, or reason. Or so he assumed.

Mary Winchester had an affair with her own brother. She kept it well hidden from her husband, though the people of Petersburg easily saw through her veil. It wasn't until her death that Robert came to realize the truth, and see that the boy he had raised from an infant—from the day of birth—was Jacob's. Enraged by his wife's betrayal, he removed Isaac from the will. To Robert, he was a reminder of infidelity, and not someone that should carry out the Winchester name. Thus, the estate was left solely to his adopted sons: William and Peter.

William, having endured the last years of Isaac's ridicule and disdain, took advantage of his new inheritance, and banished Isaac from the home. He sneered at his adoptive brother's misfortune and offered the servants' house on the other end of the property as an option for his lodging—only after Peter begged he stay. Enraged by his brother's greed and pride, he took the offer, and moved in promptly, leaving the mansion he had been born into behind him.

William denied Isaac any sort of key to the house. He would be allowed over for dinners—as a guest—but only at his discretion. *Doors*, Isaac was told, *will keep you out of my house. As long as you don't have a key, you can't get in without my blessing, and my hand.* While Peter argued that Isaac was family and deserved a rightful place amongst the house as he pleased, William denied it.

"He's no family of ours," he'd say. "He doesn't share our blood. He doesn't share anyone's blood."

After a year of living in isolation on the opposite end of the property, Isaac decided to confront his brothers. He knew that he could at least get through to Peter, but William was going to be harder to convince. As the day turned to evening, Isaac headed over to the mansion, lantern in hand, to discuss his living conditions and, as he hoped, passage to the house.

William wasn't home when he arrived, but Peter was there. And, of course, upon seeing his brother on the doorstep, he immediately welcomed him in.

"I don't understand William," Peter confessed. "You're our brother, regardless of blood. We should all be together."

Isaac agreed and explained his distress for living in the servants' house—away from the only home he knew. The home that was his mother's. He had a place in the will once, a place he had seen and had been promised since birth. William, he said, never had a place. While Peter was going to slightly agree, but also defend his biological brother's position, William returned home.

The Winchester house was filled with nothing but threats and hollers that night. Isaac lashed out at William, spewing his hatred for him and his tainted blood—blood that should never have belonged in the estate. In return, William spat back that Isaac was worthless, something that his own father had seen. William was the prized child now—the chosen heir to the fortune—and Isaac was acting infantile in not seeing it and letting it go. But again, Isaac demanded that William give him what he deserved.

"This is my mother's house!"

The slap that met Isaac's cheek echoed through the halls. William wasn't going to have any more, and he let his brother know it. *This home isn't yours*, he snarled. *Not anymore. And from this day on, my doors will always be closed to you…*

The next morning, the authorities were on the doorstep of the estate, a few items in their hands: Isaac's watch, wallet, and an envelope. The police said they found the belongings beside the train tracks just east of the village, near the crossing where the Beeding and Petersburg lines connected. William said he knew the lines well: they were the two his adoptive father had stocks in—he would frequent that location, watching the trains come in with the boys when they were younger.

But, Isaac's personal items weren't all the police found.

What was left of Isaac Winchester was mashed into the tracks, making it impossible to decipher who he was had it not been for his identification. His entrails, as the authorities said, were strewn all the way to the next county, down the Petersburg line.

Peter had already burst into tears upon hearing this information. William, on the other hand, stood with a straight face and took the belongings when they were offered.

"The only thing we can't understand," the police said before leaving that morning, "is that your brother was obviously ran over last night. But, you say he was here until when?"

"About eight." William said.

Everyone in Petersburg knew that the last train made its way into the station at sunset. No trains in autumn ran past 6pm.

Once William was able to get Peter to calm down, he went through the items the police had fetched from alongside the tracks. All had been carefully removed and placed where they would be safe—as if Isaac had been awaiting his fate. The wallet and watch made sense to William, but the envelope, addressed to him, was unexpected. Peeling it open, William read the letter he found carefully inserted inside.

"I don't *need* your doors any more to get into *my* house."

William scoffed and crumpled up the paper quickly after that. In his opinion, Isaac had gotten what was coming to him.

101

The years of torment and disrespect he had for his adopted brother finally caught up. While the threat left goosebumps across William's skin, he ignored it and headed to the parlor to begin his daily routine.

Isaac's burial was held a few days later. The authorities had managed to scrape what they could of him off the tracks for the coffin. *We're certain there's more,* they told William and Peter, *but with how gruesome it was, there's no way we'll ever be able to get all of him up.*

Peter stood beside his brother's coffin as it was lowered into the ground, tossing a single rose on top. William, on the other hand, stood off in the distance, watching with disdain. When the others had cleared out, he approached and stared down into the hole where the coffin now rested. From his pocket, he removed the crumpled letter Isaac had written to him, then dropped it in.

"Keep your threats," he hissed, and sealed his adoptive brother's grave with a wad of spit.

The family fortune continued to flourish over the years and in time, William married—Isabelle Proctor—a young woman from Beeding. Together, they had a son, Benjamin, whom William loved more than life itself. Peter remained at the estate, unmarried, to help care for Benjamin when William and Isabelle were away on the rail lines, looking to further invest in their stocks. Benjamin came to love his uncle and the lavish lifestyle he was born into. And, the east wing of the estate, where he took up residence.

When Benjamin turned ten, that all changed. He appeared one night at the foot of his father's bed, trembling and nudging him awake. William was frustrated by his son's childish behavior and sudden "fear" for the east wing of the home. He ridiculed the boy and beckoned him to go back to bed. But when Benjamin pulled a crumpled piece of paper from his night shirt pocket, William's blood went cold.

It was covered in the soil used to burry Isaac all those years ago, but even beneath the dirt and dust, the words could be seen.

"I don't *need* your doors any more to get into *my* house."

In that moment, William felt the same fear as his son.

"Uncle Isaac is angry…"

William had never told Benjamin about Isaac—the true heir to the Winchester estate. He removed as much evidence as possible of his adoptive brother's existence from the home and never spoke his name. Yet, each night, Benjamin would come into his father's room, pale and trembling, telling him that his Uncle Isaac was growing angrier and angrier. *He doesn't let me sleep… He keeps watching me.*

Peter was convinced that Isaac's return was due to not being given a proper burial. The authorities had said that they couldn't get all of him off the tracks—leaving pieces of him behind and unable to rest. William just brushed it off and told his brother it was foolish to believe in spirits. He explained that Benjamin most likely found what little was left in the house of Isaac's and he was making stories up. *The east wing* was *Isaac's quarter of the house*, he would say, *so it's likely something of his was left behind.* Of course, that didn't explain the crumpled note that was retrieved from the boy. But William continued to deny his adoptive brother's return.

A few weeks later, in the night, William and Isabelle awoke to the sounds of Benjamin screaming. They rushed to their son's bedroom, only to find him in the hall—a bloody corpse. He'd been torn apart, entrails stretching the length of the east wing. William vomited at the sight, sheltering a sobbing Isabelle's eyes. Down the hallway, written upon every wall and door, he could make out scribbled text—in Benjamin's blood.

    I don't need your doors any more.

    I don't *need* your doors any more.

    I don't *need* your *doors* any more.

    I DON'T *NEED* YOUR *DOORS* ANY MORE TO GET INTO *MY* HOUSE.

    The doors in the east wing corridor violently threw themselves open, and Isabelle screamed.

It was only a few months later that William was found dead. He had been in the parlor, where he spent most of his time, seated in his chair with a look of terror on his face. There were no wounds to be found on the body, making the authorities believe he died from a sudden heart attack. He was taken to the Petersburg Cemetery and buried alongside his adoptive father—a plot he had chosen years before.

Peter, emotionally distraught after the death of his biological brother, decided to head west. He told Isabelle he could no longer live on the estate—there had been too many deaths there: his adoptive mother and father, Isaac, Benjamin, and now William. With no heirs of his own, Peter put the land up for sale and promptly gathered what he could. Isabelle agreed to join him, and later married him. The two took the first train out in the morning. They would have left sooner, but Peter reminded Isabelle that no trains ran after 6pm.

The house remained vacant for years, until an elderly couple moved in in the late 50s. They admitted to hearing noises from the east wing of the house: doors opening and closing, and the occasional creaking, but they ignored it. *It's an old house*, they told themselves, *old houses do that*. It was only after they began to hear the shouting and things thrown around—shattering—that they moved out. They claimed two young men were always arguing, and they couldn't sleep at night.

Another family moved in not too long afterward, with a teenaged son. The boy took up residence in the east wing and would complain about hearing the arguments through the night, as well. His parents only questioned him, however, when he started sleeping in his car at night.

"This is Isaac's house," he would tell his parents. "He's not happy. He wants us to leave."

Of course, the family thought their son had been watching too many scary films, but when they found him dangling from the ceiling fan in his bedroom, note pinned to the front of his shirt, they believed him.

"This is *my* home."

A couple of years ago, a husband and wife moved into the estate, looking to turn it into a bed and breakfast. The town denied their request, simply because there wouldn't be sufficient parking, and the estate had become an historic landmark—only one of the homes surviving from the turn of the century. Thus, the couple made the mansion their home. They always found it odd, however, that their children never visited—stating that they hated the house. *When you're gone, we won't sell it*, they said, *we want absolutely nothing to do with it.*

But the couple continue to live there, content at the lavish life the estate offers. They claim, when questioned, that they hear noises from the east wing, but the hollers have long since calmed down. They said surprisingly, they seemed to vanish after Peter Winchester was brought back to Petersburg after his death in the west, to be buried alongside his brother William. *William's soul must have gone to rest once his brother passed on*, they'd say. *The two boys are together again, and that's all that matters.*

Yet, the strangest thing about the couple always comes when they are questioned about the house: How did you come to own it?

"Oh, we're not the *owners*," they always say. "We're simply the caretakers."

"Master Isaac owns the estate," they tell people. "It *was* his mother's house, after all. Now, it's a place of his own."

The people of Petersburg say that if you wander near the tracks late at night, after the trains have stopped running, there's a cool breeze that follows you, taking you to the crossroad where the lines meet. If you stand there long enough, looking through the darkness, they say you can feel sorrow, rising up from the tracks.

If you turn over your shoulder, you'll notice a well-dressed young man standing there, removing his wallet, watch, and an envelope from his pocket. He'll join you at your side, staring into the nothingness. And he'll speak not a word.

In the distance, the sound of an approaching train will rise up. You'll feel the tracks tremble as the young man steps out, only to be clipped by the fast, oncoming engine that appears to come out of nowhere. There are no cries as his body is mashed beneath the wheels, but some say there is laughter. Once the train passes and you look out at the tracks, there is nothing there. No body, no blood, no remains. And there is no train. Yet, you can still hear it, rattling along the tracks, into the night.

If you long for a peaceful walk to Beeding, feel free to cross over the Petersburg tracks at the crossroads. You may look twice, both ways, before crossing the tracks if you must, but it's not necessary—even if you hear the sound of wheels along them.
    Remember: no trains run after 6pm.

The Haunting of Berkeley Square

Berkeley Square was the darkest corner of London. It wasn't simply that the trees shaded the streets on the edges of the park or that the street lamps never blazed when twilight fell. No, there were hushed whispers throughout Mayfair of a curse. When the sun set, shadows stretched across the streets and something awoke. Had it not been for the cases of suicide and the descent into madness from previous owners, one would simply say it was a myth. But year after year, the residents of Mayfair watched as the estate of Berkeley chased out its inhabitants, and relocated them into wards. Berkeley Square truly was the darkest and most haunted corner of London.

Mayfair, London, England—1841

"It's perfect." Percy Bennett said, gripping the smooth wood of the railing.

"Indeed. It's large enough to host parties and, of course, when we're ready to start a family. Not to mention the beautiful study upstairs in the attic. I'm certain you could get most of your writings done up there." Percy's wife Emma touched his arm gently. "We'll take it."

It wasn't long before Percy and Emma moved to Berkeley Square, inviting guests over for dinner on the weekends. Each week, they would arrive in their carriages, dressed in waist coats and expensive gowns to discuss the future of what would be the Bennett family.

"We were planning travelling sometime in the spring. Percy says that we should take our holiday in Paris! Such a grand history France has, and I'm certain it will be inspirational for his newest piece." Emma conversed all night with the other young women of Mayfair. "Percy's had his hopes up for some time to get a serial of his work out, perhaps in *Ainsworth's*. He still thinks he'll be the next great Byron or Shelley. Literature of the Gothic has *always* been Percy's niche. Ah! Speaking of, here he comes now."

Percy hurried down the stairwell, adjusting his jacket. He smirked somewhat, heading towards Emma before taking her hand and planting a kiss against her knuckles.

"My apologies for running late. You know how it can be when I'm trying to finish a chapter."

"I understand." Emma smiled.

Just as his wife had, Percy began conversing with the guests of his current works and plans for the future. He mentioned travels he longed to take as well as places he had already been. Yet, the majority of his conversation remained with his closest friend Jonathon around the novel he had been writing. The story of a young woman who was tormented by life and slowly slipping into madness.

"Is that why you chose to live here?" Jonathon asked. "I was rather surprised when I heard you had taken up the offer."

"What do you mean?"

"Oh, come now, Percy. Surely you've heard of the 'curse' of Berkeley before."

Percy was silent for a moment. "No, I'm afraid I haven't."

The group around Percy silenced themselves as Jonathon looked him over. His eyebrow was raised in disbelief, yet, he continued on with the story just the same. By now, everyone that had gathered around to listen.

"Legend has it that a young woman used to live here years ago with her uncle. His long hours of work made the young woman's uncle start to go somewhat mad. He began abusing her; physically and mentally. After she threatened to go to the law, he locked her in the attic. And, it was from there that she jumped from the window and committed suicide on the streets below. Some say she went mad from the abuse and isolation. Others say she was just trying to seek help and make it to the law. People say strange sounds can be heard from the attic at night, and those who live up there will go insane, possibly to the point of suicide themselves."

Emma bit her lip. "I've never heard of such a tale before. I-is that... Jonathon, is that true?"

"Of *course* it's not true!" Percy laughed. "Come now, Jonathon. I do all of my work in the attic. I've turned it into my study and I've yet to come across a ghost."

"Believe what you want." Jonathon shrugged. "But word of this...*myth* is spreading. Just keep your eyes open up there, lest it be true."

After clapping Percy on the shoulder, Jonathon turned to walk away. He nodded to Emma with a smile before heading towards the door. Percy wrapped an arm around Emma, he pulled her against him, whispering.

"It's just a legend…"

Percy dipped his quill into the inkwell. He was nearing the end of his leatherback journal and knew that before the month was up he would have to invest in a new one. The afternoon light from the attic window streamed across his desk. He stopped only when the sound of footsteps ascended up the stairs.

"I thought you refused to come up here." Percy said once Emma stood in the doorway, carrying a tray with tea and biscuits.

"Well, I figured you needed to take a break." Emma set the tray beside Percy. "You've been up here all day."

"I've been motivated."

Emma caressed Percy's shoulders, then leaned in and kissed him. Percy chuckled at the touch.

"Promise me you won't forget to come down for dinner again tonight, Percy. I'm afraid one of these nights you're just going to stay up here and never come back downstairs. They say writing's been known to drive people to insanity if they think about it too much." Emma said softly once she pulled away.

"As has worrying. I'll be fine."

It was around 3AM when Emma awoke in a cold sweat. At first, she thought she was hearing things, but when the floorboards creaked above her head, she nudged Percy. He moaned in aggravation, lifting his head to glance at her.

"What is it?"

Emma hushed him as she waited for the next sound to rise, but all was silent. Percy rolled over in an attempt to fall back asleep. It was only when the floorboards creaked again and a low whimper came from above that he raised his head from his pillow. There was another pause before the next sound: a pained howl.

"Percy…" Emma gripped the sheets tightly in her hands. "It's coming from the attic."

Percy pulled the covers off and swung his feet onto the cold floor. He reached for the oil lamp beside his bed, lighting it. Emma watched in horror as he got to his feet with the lamp, heading towards the stairwell.

"I'm certain it's nothing."

"Percy! Don't! What if—?"

"I work all day up there, Emma. There's nothing up there, trust me."

Again, Emma called for him as he ascended the stairwell into the darkness. The stairs creaked under Percy's feet as he pushed through the doorway to his study. Shadows stretched across the floor from the light of the lamp. Percy allowed his eyes to adjust to the darkness, creating shapes where his belongings were.

The lamp flickered as Percy scanned the interior. It was only when he turned to head back downstairs that he spotted something move in the corner of his eye—something white. Percy tilted his head in the direction of the movement, raising the lamp to get a better view. The curtain pulled across the window blew softly in the wind, creating a whistle through the cracks. Setting the lamp on his desk, he moved the curtain away, shutting the window for the night.

"I just forgot to latch the window." Percy explained to Emma once he was back in bed. "It was just the wind. I'm certain that's all the creaks were."

Percy wrapped his arms around her before kissing her forehead. "You worry too much. Don't let Jonathon's ghost stories frighten you. There's nothing up there. It's all in your head.

"Alice drowns herself," Percy explained to Emma over afternoon tea. His leatherback journal lay opened in his lap as he sipped tea, scanning his story. "I haven't concluded a reason yet, perhaps something over marriage or an engagement gone wrong, but at least I'm certain about that part."

"You said she haunts the river where she drowned, yes?" Emma asked.

"I wouldn't necessarily call it *haunting*. I see it more that they want something from those who are still living. To me, haunting is about for revenge. Alice's not like that. She just wants help."

"Someone to help her find her way to the afterlife, I presume?" Emma raised an eyebrow as she set her teacup down.

"I suppose you could say that. Or perhaps she's just waiting for her lover."

Percy continued writing into the late hours of evening. Ink had splotched in some areas of the page due to his exhaustion, but he knew he had to keep writing. There were only a few chapters left now, leading up to Alice's eventual peace.

"...amber ringlets of hair wet from the river. Alice rose again to greet the young man on the banks. She longed for his poetry, how they reminded her of her past love; the love that abandoned her and led her to her grave beneath the ripples. Now, only his words could set her free."

Percy ran his hands over his face, his eyes weary from the dim light and small text which now stared back at him like foreign symbols. He was almost finished. Rubbing his eyes, Percy removed the quill from his inkwell once more.

Percy noticed the flame in his oil lamp begin to dim. He peered up from his work, glancing over to examine the lighting. Yet, his eyes didn't catch the flicker trapped behind the glass. Instead, they fell upon the reflection of a young woman. It was only for a brief moment that he saw her, skin pale and almost blending in with her white dress. Even her wavy amber hair appeared to fade into the flame. Percy looked over his shoulder into the darkness, but no one was there. Slapped the cover of his journal shut, Percy went down to bed. He knew exhaustion was getting the better of him.

"You're positive you haven't seen anything?" Jonathon pressed at the gathering Percy and Emma prepared for Christmas.

Through sips of his wine, Percy nodded. "We've been here for almost four months now, Jonathon, and no; there's nothing to speak of."

"Well, there are some noises at night." Emma corrected as she looked to Percy. "They come from the attic, but Percy says that it's nothing. Just the wind."

"I often forget to latch the window. It gets awfully stuffy up there." Percy added before turning his head to cough. It was deeper than he expected.

"Even now, in winter?" Jonathon looked suspicious.

"I'd say the wind now is simply coming in through the gaps in the wood around the window or something. I can feel it every once in a while at my desk blowing in, that's for sure. Blows the pages of my journal and puts the candle out sometimes."

Clearing his throat, Jonathon put an arm around Percy's shoulders, leading him away. He spoke under his breath to avoid others around him from hearing.

"So, how exactly is that novel of yours coming along?"

"I thought I was doing rather well lately, but these past few days I've barely gotten a word in. Honestly, I sit in that attic all day just staring at my journal."

Jonathon made sure no one was looking before reaching into his coat pocket and removing a small glass bottle. "I can help with that."

He slipped it into Percy's hands. Spinning the bottle around to read the label, Percy raised an eyebrow, stuttering at what he read.

"*Laudanum?*"

"I know it's usually only prescribed as a pain killer or for insomnia patients needing sleep, but I do believe that it could help you finish what you need."

"You want me to take *laudanum* to inspire me?" Percy's voice had risen now, and Jonathon was insistent on hushing him.

"You said yourself you wanted to be the next great. How do you think they managed to get their ideas and complete them? Laudanum's done wonders for the mind, Percy."

"But... Jonathon..."

"Just a small dose here and there. It won't hurt. If anything, it will help you focus for a few hours or at least inspire you enough to continue. On top of that..." Jonathon leaned in closer to Percy, whispering against his ear. "Don't think that cough of yours isn't noticeable. Consumption's been targeting the masses. I hear they're calling it the "White Plague" or something now. You can never be too sure."

Percy stared down at the bottle as Jonathon's hands slid away from his shoulders. The liquid sloshed within as he continued to gaze upon the label. Biting his lip, he tucked it away within his jacket pocket, watching as Jonathon nodded with a smirk.

"I look forward to reading you in *Ainsworth's*."

The laudanum was bitter on Percy's tongue as the first swig went down. He scrunched up his nose, grimacing at the flavor before pushing the cork back into the top of the bottle and emitting a cough. He wasn't certain how long it took for the effect to show, but nevertheless began writing a few notes on the back page of his journal.

"Vengeful." Percy drew circles around the word with his quill tip, as he thought aloud. "Haunting. What if those were

Alice's true intentions for the poet? No… she's a good spirit." He pushed his palms to his forehead with a groan. "She's not vengeful… She simply longs for love."

The flame within the lamp flickered once more and Percy couldn't help but squint once it came into his vision. The light was almost too intense for him as he felt a twinge in his temples. The pain was sharp at first, but then drowned itself out, but continued to resurface in waves.

He leaned forward over the desk, gripping his temples with closed eyes, attempting to drown the pain out. Under his breath, he cursed the toxin. Yet, it was the laudanum that made him open his eyes and sit up once more. Percy read the label over again, remembering its prescribed use as a painkiller. Surely it would help with the headache he thought, taking another gulp of the bitter liquid. This time, Percy didn't grimace. Instead, he picked up his quill and began filling in the gaps of his text.

After his small burst of inspiration, Percy began to feel the drowsiness. His eyelids became heavy and he could no longer focus on the page before him. When he finally closed them, leaning over his journal from exhaustion, was when he heard it. A soft crying rose up from behind him, causing him to steadily reopen his eyes and gaze over his shoulder.

There, standing behind him, was a young woman. Her hair fell in matted auburn ringlets and her white dress was partially torn and smeared with light blood. At first, Percy was taken aback, jolting at the sight of her. Nevertheless, she approached, drying her tears as she held an arm out to him.

"W-wait! Please… don't go…" Her voice sounded almost familiar to Percy as he watched her, still trembling. "Your stories… I like listening to them. You read aloud, you know? When you think. I think it's lovely."

Percy didn't know if it was his curiosity or the laudanum which kept him from running. From screaming. Yet, he didn't move from his desk. Instead, he remained silent for a few more moments, until finally gathering the courage to shakily speak.

"W-why, thank you." He tried to keep his eyes averted, but something kept making him look back at the woman standing there. "May… I ask how long you… how long you've been listening? Overhearing my stories, at least."

"Since you came here," the woman replied. "I watched you move in up here a few months ago. I was suspicious of what kind of man you were. What talents you possessed… what secrets. We all have secrets, don't we? Things we keep hidden inside us. When we're alone, that's when we seem to let them out."

Percy was silent.

"I know your secret, Mr. Bennett." She smiled at him. "You're sick, the early stages, but still. You know you are… and you don't want anyone to find out. I also know that you want to complete that story of yours before you *literally* become consumed by your illness."

"I've had hardly any motivation or inspiration…"

The woman approached Percy, causing him to freeze up. "I can help you with that. We all know our secrets are just hidden desires, and that's what you want more than anything. To complete your story. I can help, Mr. Bennett."

"And…how could you possibly do that?"

"Why, I already know your entire story. You *do* talk in your sleep quite often. All it would take is some annotation from me, and you'll have your draft completed by the end of the month. Guaranteed."

The offer certainly was tempting. Yet, Percy wasn't sure who this woman was. Was she just in his head; a figment of his imagination brought on by the laudanum, or perhaps he truly was just dreaming? Or, was she real; a woman who had found her way into the attic to listen to his stories? Or…

The feeling of dread began to rise in him.

"My uncle used to read me stories when I was a little girl. That was before he went mad and locked me up here. It was terrible." The woman looked as if she were about to cry again. "It was an accident what happened… he kept blaming me when the law came and took him away. I watched them do it. But, even after the accident happened, I never really felt free."

"Free?"

She nodded. "That's my secret I suppose; my greatest desire. I want someone to set me free."

Percy looked at her sadly. "If only there were a way I could help. Perhaps, if you help me with my story, I'll be able to try and help you out. Yes?"

"You… you would set me free of this place?"

Percy nodded. "Yes. In the best way that I can."

"You mustn't tell your wife. A-about any of this. I've heard how she speaks of me an—"

"Considering how horrified she is of Jonathon's "tales", I wouldn't dream of doing such a thing. Seems you'll be becoming my newest secret."

He hugged his journal against his chest at the thought, watching as the young woman smiled to him. "Thank you, Mr. Bennett."

As she turned to walk away, steadily fading with each movement she made, Percy couldn't help but call out to her. "Wait! I didn't get your name."

The woman stopped once again, glancing back over her shoulder at Percy as she smirked. Percy was certain he saw the flame from the lamp flicker in her eye.

"Alice."

"You've been acting rather odd." Emma carefully watched Percy skim the pages of his journal as he sat propped up in bed.

"Odd?" His vision never met hers.

"You've been missing dinner again. And I hardly ever see you downstairs. Is everything alright?"

Percy folded the cover of the journal closed. "Everything's fine. Honestly."

"You've been muttering Alice's name in your sleep."

"I'm fine."

"As long as you're sure." Emma whispered, moving against Percy for comfort. "I just hate seeing you locked up in the attic all day and night. It can't be good for you. I'm worried you'll end up going—"

"Mad?"

There was silence.

"I want to leave, Percy. I know you love it here, but…"

"I need to finish, Emma."

"Must it be here?"

"I worry elsewhere it never will be finished. *This* is where it must be done. I'm so close, Emma, and I've been inspired these past few days. I've stressed enough over it; don't take that last bit of motivation away."

Emma sighed and burrowed her head into the pillow. Reaching up, she tenderly stroked Percy's face, brushing strands of his hair away. He simply stared down at her, not moving.

"I just want you to finish your work Percy, but finish it without worrying too much of it. It's not healthy to be caught up entirely in fantasy. You forget what's real and what matters. I want you to be able to complete what you've been striving for all these months, so that you can hopefully get it out there somewhere and we can finally move to the country and settle down and be able to start a family. That's all I've wanted, Percy, and I know that's what you want, as well."

Percy looked her over once again, leaning in and kissing her, running his hands down her shoulders. She tasted sweet against the fresh, bitter laudanum that still stained his mouth. Rolling on top of her, Percy allowed the drug to fully take control.

The floorboards creaked as Percy entered the attic later that night, the light from the moon illuminating the walls. He squinted as he made his way towards the center of the room, voice low as he approached the young woman in the flowing white dress.

"Alice?"

She turned from the window to face him, her pale skin reflecting in the faint light. Percy continued to approach her, watching as her hands slipped from the windowsill. It was then he noticed the blood stains across her chest, from the suicide he presumed. Her light blue eyes were almost piercing questions as they observed him, yet, she didn't speak.

"I've never asked you before, but have been meaning to. Why do you still wait up here?" Percy's voice was low. "Is it for him?"

The woman was silent for a moment longer, but then answered. "I wait for the one that will take me from this place.

There are memories here that I wish could be forgotten. Surely you understand."

"You make it nearly impossible to write." Percy said as he watched her. "I know your intentions are pure, but there are times when you distract me from my work. The pacing and crying..."

"If it weren't for me, you'd hardly have *anything* complete, Percy." Alice approached him, taking hold of his hand. She was cold to the touch, but Percy didn't shudder. He simply allowed her to continue. "I inspire you, admit it. You birthed me from your words and made me all that I am, thus I am here when you are at a loss for them. That was our deal, remember?"

Percy smirked as he gazed into Alice's eyes before leaning in and kissing her. Just as her hands were, her lips shared the same icy feel. Unlike Emma's, however, they were bitter, tasting vaguely of laudanum. Yet again, he didn't pull away. He drowsily watched her fade in and out as she smiled back at him through his lightheadedness. The sleeves of his shirt were now stained with the same blood that was across her chest, causing him to glance down at it before being drawn back to her.

"Be my poet, Percy. Take me away from this place. Leave her and together we can build your fantasy; make it reality."

There was a pause, but Percy finally shook his head. "I can't, Alice."

"But, you promised me. Promised you would set me free!"

"Oh, Alice...Only words can set you free."

Percy awoke on the attic floor the next morning, his journal sprawled out next to him. His head throbbed in agony, vision still blurred from the dosage of laudanum he had taken the night before. As he sat up, he noticed the now dried blood on his sleeves, causing him to shake his head in alarm. Nevertheless, he popped the cork free from the bottle and took another sip in an attempt to drown the pain before rising to his feet and heading downstairs.

"Emma?"

There was nothing but silence throughout the house and even before Percy entered the kitchen, empty, with no breakfast prepared, did he find it odd. He called out for her again, heading towards the bedroom in hopes she had simply overslept. Prying the doorway open, Percy peered in, only to be taken aback by the horrific sight displayed.

Blood soaked the sheets of the bed where Emma's body lay. Her throat was slit in a clean line, as if it had been a ribbon of blood tied around her neck. Resting beside her was the blade which did the crime, glinting with the ruby droplets of lost life. Percy staggered into the room without words as he fell to his knees beside her, staring down upon her lifeless and pale face.

"Emma..."

He reached out to her, stroking her bloodstained strands of hair as he attempted to blink the tears from his eyes. His throat and chest burned from disbelief and he continued to shake his head, pressing it to hers before trembling.

"Why? Emma, how did… I don't understand."

From the attic above, Alice's laughter could be heard. Raising his head from Emma's, Percy narrowed his eyes bitterly, pulling away from her. Jonathon's words continued to litter his mind, of insanity and suicide, while Alice's longing for Percy to leave his wife overpowered them. Clenching his fists, he stormed up the stairwell.

Percy locked the door leading up to the attic before downing what was left in the bottle of laudanum. Once inside, Alice's laughter continued to pierce his ears.

"How could you?"

"Oh, Percy, it wasn't me who took her from you. She simply went insane, just like all the others."

"No!" Percy shot back. "I know what you did. You wanted me to leave her so that you could have me for yourself. You'll never have me, Alice."

Alice stopped her mocking laughter as Percy tugged his journal out, glancing over to the oil lamp on the desk. He walked towards it, removing the glass casing before holding the cover above the flame, the edges beginning to catch fire steadily.

"What are you doing?" Alice cried out.

"You said you wanted me to set you free, and that's simply what I'm doing. Freeing you and myself from this nightmare."

Once the fire stretched across the cover of the journal, Percy threw it to the floor of the attic, watching as the pages slowly began to turn to ash. Taking one final glimpse at Alice, he threw the oil lamp next. The attic blazed in the flames that licked the walls and Alice's screams rose up from the smoke as Percy closed his eyes, allowing the laudanum to send him into his burning dreamland for the last time.

Mayfair, London, England—1880

"It's perfect." A young man turned to his wife with a smile as he glanced up the stairwell.

His wife nodded back, holding their infant in her arms. "That it is. A wonderful place to raise a family. We'll take it."

No one told them of the hushed whispers of Berkeley Square. The people of Mayfair spoke of a spirit who had gone mad in life. A writer who locked himself away in an attic while illusions slowly drove him to madness. It was said he murdered his wife before committing suicide in the attic by burning his journal filled with the very writings that caused his insanity. Some said at night, voices could be heard from the attic and all who enter will suffer the same fate. However, whether fact or fiction, one thing was true to those who lived in Mayfair.

Berkeley Square truly was the darkest, and most haunted corner of London.

ABOUT THE AUTHOR

Dorian J. Sinnott is a graduate of Emerson College's Writing, Literature, and Publishing program, currently residing in the beautiful and historic Kingston, NY with his two cats. He spends his weekends cosplaying at comic cons up and down the east coast, and herding cats at his local animal shelter. Dorian's work has appeared in numerous magazines and journals aside from those featured in this anthology, including: *Crab Fat Literary Magazine, The Cabinet of Heed,* and *Soft Cartel.*

Printed in Great Britain
by Amazon